LEGION of the Sky

Book One in the Journeys of Septimus Legion

Samuel L. Larsen

ISBN: 978-1-69769583-0

Front and back cover images by Lauren Larsen
Book design by Samuel L. Larsen

Printed by Kindle Direct Publishing in the United States of America.

First printing edition 2019.

This is Samuel Larsen's first published work.

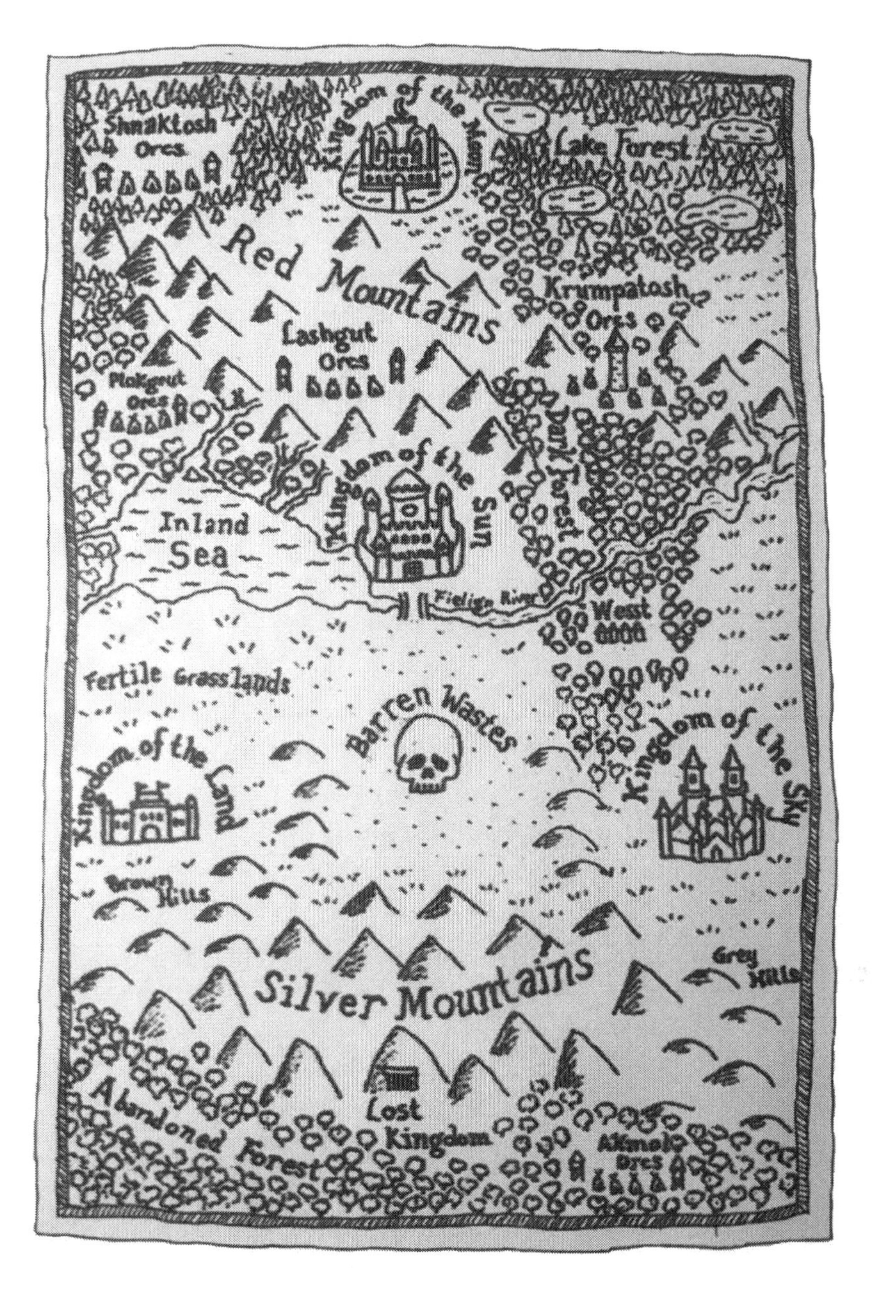

Julius Aurelius' Map of the Known World

Prologue

The poets say that at the beginning of time, the first settlers of the world were divided into five nations. The most powerful being was the Creator, and he chose a king for each of the five nations. There were two kingdoms of Elves, one kingdom of Men, one kingdom of Halflings, and one kingdom of Orcs.

The Creator asked each king what name their kingdoms would be called by, and then promised a gift to match the name they chose. The first king to step forward was one of the kings of Elves, and he boldly asserted that his kingdom would be called The Kingdom of the Sky. The Creator nodded and said that in that case their gift would be swiftness and agility.

The second king to step forward was the king of Men. He had thought more deeply about this and chose the name of The Kingdom of the Sun. The Creator nodded once again and said that their gift would be the power of light, and his people would dispel the darkness before them.

The third king to step forward might have actually been the second in line, but he was so small he wasn't noticed until the king of Men had finished speaking. The third king was, of course, the king of the Halflings. He said his kingdom would be called the Kingdom of the Land. The Creator smiled and said that their gift would be skill with agriculture, and they would feed the hungry souls of the land.

The fourth king was angry and brooding, and when he stepped forward the others backed away. He was the king of the Orcs, and he thought it unfair that the others had claimed the skies, the sun, and the land before he could think of a name for his kingdom. He said there was nothing left but darkness, so the domains of the Orcs would be the Kingdom of Night.

The Creator sighed and then nodded reluctantly and said that his gift would be power of darkness, to counter the light, for there could be no light without darkness.

The last king smiled slyly and stepped forward with a flourishing bow. He was the second king of Elves, and he said that he would humbly choose the Kingdom of the Moon, which he acknowledged was less radiant than the splendorous Kingdom of the Sun.

But then he made a demand that was quite unexpected. "Because of this weakness I fear that we will be vulnerable to our enemies; therefore, I demand that we receive the gift of lethal power in the night, that when our enemies are weakest, we will be at the peak of our strength."

The Creator shook his head and rebuked the Elf. "It is not your right to make demands when I offer gifts. I see that in your heart you do not desire to defend your people, but rather to dominate all others. Because you have done this, your gift is a punishment that matches the evil desires of your heart. The light of the sun will always weaken your kingdom, and you will no longer be able to hide your thirst for blood from anyone." Their gift was no gift at all, but rather was the curse of vampirism.

The five kings dispersed and took their people to different quarters of the world where they established their kingdoms. According to the poets, that is how the world began in the distant past, many thousands of years ago.

Chapter One: A Midnight Escape

So this is the weirdest thing: I woke up in the middle of the night when the moon was at its highest. I arose from my bed and got dressed, quietly fastening my sword to my belt. I glanced in the mirror and saw the moonlight glinting off the tips of my ears and my purple eyes. I grimaced at my tousled, short brown hair. Okay, I had bed head, but actually it always looked like that.

Anyway...I, Septimus Legion, seventh son of King Leon, ruler of the Kingdom of the Sky, knew that I would never become king because of my standing in my family. I was fine with that. That meant I could do what I wanted, and what I wanted right now was to sneak out of the city at night and go on a quest. I didn't know what kind of quest that would be, but I could figure that out as I went.

I carefully shouldered the heavy satchel of essentials that I had packed the day before, and slipped out of my first-floor window into the castle's courtyard. As I was closing the window, I heard a soft voice behind me.

"Where do you think you're going?" It was a woman's voice.

I almost dropped my pack, but recovered quickly and turned to see a hooded figure standing near me. For a moment I thought it was my cousin, Olivia, but she had been gone for two years, and besides, it didn't sound like her.

"Sorry, I don't recognize your voice. Are you one of the new guards assigned to this wing of the castle?" I asked.

"Does your father have any guards that look like me?" She removed her hood and I saw that she had the pale face and dark hair of an Elven girl of about my age, but I had never seen her before.

Then I noticed her eyes. Was it a trick of the moonlight? Her eyes were a startling blue, like sapphires, but they seemed to shine with red-tinted light. She had her long brown hair up in a ponytail, with bangs sweeping across her forehead.

"Where are you from?" I was confused because she didn't resemble any of the Elves of the Kingdom of the Sky that I had ever met.

"I'm from a land far to the North, where you fear to go and I dare not name. I have come to seek your help, and offer you mine in exchange." She said.

"There are no Elves far to the North, just the bitter Kingdom of the Moon, and that would make you…"

"A Vampire?" She interrupted me.

"Holy catfish! Are you? But you look so much like an Elf—not like the ravenous monsters we learned to fear as children." I said.

"We were not so different from Elves once." She brushed her hair back from her ear and showed me the point, but I also noticed the sharpness of her short fangs. If you didn't know, Vampire fangs are actually shorter than you would think—the fangs just go down to the middle of their bottom teeth. (Fun fact for you there!)

"You know I could have you killed?" I pointed out. "Why are you risking your life to come here?"

"You are the seventh son of the king, with virtually no chance of ever getting the throne. And you want to go on a quest, right?"

"How would you know that?"

"And—you don't actually have a plan?"

"Of course I do! My plan is to wing it and figure things out as I go."

"Wow, that sounds like a lot of fun." She smiled. "But I can make things a little easier for you, because I already have a quest that is suited perfectly for you."

"Oh, I'm sure you do." A strange Vampire who shows up at night outside my window with the perfect quest for me? What kind of quest would that be? I imagined being led away to a waiting pack of Vampires outside the city who were waiting to suck me dry. No thanks. "You know, I could yell and call the guards right now."

She laughed. "You won't do that. Not when you're sneaking out of your bedroom window under the dark of night. Wouldn't that alert whoever it is you are sneaking away from?"

She called my bluff. Obviously, I had been bluffing, but what else could I say? "You're right." I admitted. "Hey, you know, I forgot something—I'll be right back."

I flung my window open and leapt back into my room, then shut it tight and snapped the latch close. But to my amazement, she didn't try to stop me or attack me from behind—in fact, she was nowhere to be seen.

She was gone.

Chapter Two: The Journey Begins

The next thing I knew, I woke up in my bed. I wondered if the Vampire girl had been a dream, but then I saw that I was still wearing my travelling clothes. It hadn't been a dream—but I must have gone back to sleep after she left. I arose and went quickly to the throne room where I knew I would find my father, because he was an early riser and gave audience to the people every morning.

The throne room was an enormous white marble hall, full of pillars and stained glass windows in various shades of light and dark blue. There was little furniture in the room aside from the throne on the raised platform at the end of the hall. Guards stood beside the pillars and there were few petitioners this morning who were seeking my father's judgement or help with their troubles.

My father was old, but almost as good looking as I was with his long silver hair, light green eyes, and long pointed ears. Anyways, my father was looking very noble in his silver and navy blue robes which matched his silver crown encrusted with sapphires. He sat on his throne, leaning forward and listening with interest to someone who probably had a nasty problem they wanted him to solve for them.

As I got closer I saw that he was conversing with a young woman whose back was to me, but I felt a chill run down my spine as soon as I saw her. It couldn't be the very person I came to warn him about? But as I approached closer I had no doubt. It was the Vampire girl! My father and the Vampire girl were joking and laughing about something, and I interrupted.

"Father, do you know who this is?" I asked
"Ah, good morning, Septimus! I was just talking with your charming friend here. She was telling me the funniest story about you planning to run away because you'll never be king! I'm surprised you never mentioned her before."

She told my father I was running away? Now I was really ticked off. "She's not a friend. She's a Vampire!" I said. Both my father and the girl appeared shocked by my accusation.

"I apologize for my son's rudeness. We have taught him much better manners, I assure you." He scowled at me.

"No need to apologize. It's an inside joke that Septimus and I share." She smiled sweetly, and I saw her sharp fangs again.

I could feel the heat of the redness on my face. "Father just look at her!"

He glanced at her and then back at me, and she smiled even wider. "Oh, never mind." I said in disgust. "Look, there are people waiting here about real problems. What problem did she bring you to solve?" I asked.

There was murmuring from the townspeople who seemed to agree with me.

Father sighed. "If you must know, we were just discussing your plans to visit the outer reaches of the land together with your friends. The problem is that since you don't like to plan things out in advance, you would probably end up wandering into an Orc camp." Father and the Vampire girl laughed again, and now my ears were burning with embarrassment. "But I hear you have already packed and are planning to leave today. Why didn't you tell me sooner?"

"I don't know," I stammered. The truth was that I was old enough to be on my own but since I was a prince that was out of the question, so I had been planning to run away. Before I could come up with a good excuse, the murmuring of the townspeople in the hall grew loud enough that Father noticed their impatience.

"It doesn't matter—I have duties to attend to. Enjoy your journey and make sure you have your guard with you. I can't afford to keep paying ransoms to bandits every time my children wander out of the city." Father said.

Why did he always assume that I would make a mess of things? I clenched my teeth but held my temper. "I'll take a guard and make sure I don't get kidnapped this time."

"Be sure that you do that," Father said. "And pay close attention to details and remember everything you see. I'll want a full report of your adventure when you return."

"Of course, Father."

I stomped off to my room and grabbed my satchel and my sword, but since I can't stay mad very long I was already whistling and starting to get excited about the quest before I even got there. When I was heading back to the throne room I ran into a few of the castle guards, and one of them approached me.

"Excuse me prince Septimus but we have information on your guard, Felix." The guard said.

"What about him?" I asked.

"He's still upset about how you ruined his courtship with the young Elf woman he was so fond of." The guard said.

"Oh, you mean Evangeline?" I asked.

"He knows it was you that sent her a poem and told her it was from that short, bearded fellow." The guard said.

"How did he find out? I mean, it turned out for the best, right? I heard they're going to have a lovely wedding—her and what was his name? Arnie?" I said.

The castle guard chuckled. "Felix didn't think it was for the best, and it probably wouldn't be wise to ask him to accompany you to the countryside with your friends."

"I won't ask him, I'll just tell him."

"That's probably not a good idea. He's going to say no, and maybe a few other choice words that probably shouldn't be said."

"That's insubordination! He can't refuse an order from a prince! I could have him thrown in prison for that."

The castle guards all burst out laughing. "Come now, we all know that's not going to happen. And by the way, we can't assist you either because we've been assigned to your brother, Henrik. His constant troublemaking is keeping us extremely busy. I guess you'll have to find someone else to guard you. We bid you farewell, young prince." The guard said.

The guards left in a hurry to most likely stop my younger brother from lighting fireworks in the stables. I stood there thinking for a moment when I thought. "Of course, I'll just bring my best friend to guard me—but first I'll need to get that Vampire girl."

I quickly left the corridor to the throne room to get her, and I found her waiting by my father's throne. I was a little surprised that my father was gone (most likely went to take care of my brother's mischief), while the townspeople stood and grumbled while they waited for him to return.

"Come on, we're leaving." I said to the Vampire girl. "But we need to make a stop on our way out."

"You need to get your guard to go with us?" The Vampire girl asked.

"Kind of...we're going to get my best friend instead." I said

"What happened to your guard?" The vampire girl asked.

"Felix? Um, well, you see there's a wedding taking place without him that he wanted to be part of, and it's sort of my fault, so he doesn't really like me at the moment." I said.

The Vampire girl chuckled. "Well, let's get going then." We walked out of the castle and into the town. We walked around the town until we stopped at my "guard's" house.

I used our secret knock on the front door. We heard a few loud crashes from inside the house. The door opened and it was my best friend, Demetri Smith.

He wasn't a full Elf, but he was what you would call a Half-Elf. His father was of the race of Men, and was the main blacksmith of the town. Demetri was taller than his father, about the same height as the Vampire girl and me. He had short brown hair and brown eyes, and he was wearing a white, collared shirt and a blacksmith apron.

Demetri smiled. "Allo, Septimus! Who's this?"

"According to her—and my father—she's a friend, and we are apparently going on a quest, but she won't tell me what it's about." I said.

Sierra sighed. "I'll tell you when there aren't so many listening ears about." She whispered.

"Okay, okay! So, Demetri are you coming or what?" I asked.

"Sure, color me intrigued." Demetri said. "Let me pack a bag real fast."

Demetri went back inside for about twenty minutes where we heard a lot of crashing and banging, and then came out with a pot on his head which he took off immediately after noticing it. His bag was so full, it looked as if it were going to pop. He also had his sword on his belt, but now his apron was hanging on a hook inside.

"I'm ready. Let's go." Demetri said.

I got my horse from the royal stables and when I returned Sierra had a horse (I'm assuming it was the one she came here with), and Demetri had borrowed one of his father's horses. We rode through the town and out through the gates before I stopped beyond the earshot of the sentries at the gate. I didn't know where we were headed.

"You said you have a quest that was perfect for me. So where are we going…actually I don't even know your name." I said.

Demetri laughed. "Septimus, you're telling me we're going on a quest with this girl and you don't even know her name?"

The Vampire girl smiled. "My name is Sierra Evans."

I was frozen with shock. "Wait, you're the princess of the Vampires?!"

Demetri was surprised by my question. "She's a Vampire??"

Sierra looked around to make sure nobody had overheard us. "Shush! All will be explained, but we need to get to the next town called Wesst, then we will stay at the Red Sky Inn. Once we get there I will tell you what's going on, do you understand?" Sierra said exasperatedly.

Demetri and I both nodded, but I was concerned. Wesst was nearly a two day ride, and we weren't going to find out what our quest was about until then? But Sierra was already riding away, so we followed her toward the town of Wesst.

Chapter Three: The First Challenge

We rode until it was close to nightfall talking the whole time about the crazy adventures that Demetri and I and my cousin, Olivia, had had in the past (which often ended up with us getting injured or kidnapped by bandits, and my father had to pay a ransom to get us back). Sierra laughed at our stories, but didn't share much about her own background, other than the fact that she had traveled widely through several kingdoms.

We dismounted in a small grassy valley near the edge of a forest, then set up the two tents Sierra had brought with her. We had a little trouble setting up the tents because the posts didn't want to stand up straight and the oilskin kept falling down. Sierra had to show us the technique for getting them to stay up, and told us the posts were unique to her kingdom. She said they had been made out of the hollow and flimsy bones of the giants who used to rule the world (before the creator wiped them out and brought our settlers to this land). I didn't know if I believed her. Whatever they were made of, they weren't ideal tent posts, except for the fact that they were lightweight and easier to carry than wooden posts.

After we set up the tents we lit a small campfire, had a meal, and slept fitfully on the hard ground in our tents. Early the next morning we arose and started a new campfire, but just then I heard a whiny voice nearby I hadn't heard in a long time—Victor! He was a notorious criminal in this part of the land, and it sounded like he was talking to one of his henchmen in the woods nearby.

"Quiet!" I whispered to Demetri and Sierra, who were joking and laughing while they were taking down the clumsy tents.

"What is it?" Demetri whispered to me.

"Listen!" I whispered back. We listened to the voices again. "You know who that is?"

"Oh no, Victor! We've got to pack up and go!" Demetri whispered.

"Wait, who is Victor?" Sierra asked, as we carefully and quietly broke camp and saddled our horses.

"Victor is a criminal who captures people and holds them hostage until someone pays the ransom. My father has had to pay him a dozen times, but Victor always escapes justice when the soldiers go after him. He has never been caught!" I whispered.

"Wait, Sierra, don't you have Vampire powers?" I asked.

"Yes, but, I can't—"

I was confused. "What are we worried about? You could probably handle a bunch of ruffians!"

"Yeah, I would love to see you use your Vampire magic on these guys!" Demetri grinned.

"No, you don't understand—my powers don't work right now!" she whispered.

"Why not? Are you saying your powers are broken?" Demetri asked.

"That's not too far off, but I'll explain later! Let's just get out of here!" Sierra whispered.

Everything was packed and loaded, and we were about to put out the fire when Victor and his henchmen came out of the forest with their swords drawn.

"Allo Septimus! Fancy meeting you here." Victor said.

"Hello Victor. To tell you the truth, I don't fancy it all." Sierra climbed up on her horse while Demetri and I drew our swords. "Stay back or I'll wound you!" Demetri said, and then added, "Mortally!"

Victor and his men laughed. "You lads are scary!" He scoffed. "Too bad you didn't bring any real men with you for protection. Get 'em!"

He and his men approached us, but just then Demetri ran right into the campfire and kicked the blackened logs with his heavy leather boot. Flaming embers flew up and sprayed Victor and his ruffians in the face. Sierra was already riding away when we leapt onto our horses and dug in our heels, spurring horses into a gallop before Victor and his henchmen could catch us.

Chapter Four: The Red Sky Inn

We rode hard for a while, continually looking over our shoulders because we were afraid that we were being followed. After several miles the horses were foaming and wheezing and we had to slow our pace. We came to a stream in a wooded area where we stopped briefly to let the horses water, then we walked the horses up the stream for a long ways before we returned to the road. Thankfully there was no sign of Victor.

We rode cautiously for the rest of the day and finally arrived at the town called Wesst just before nightfall. We left our exhausted horses at the town stables, and then Sierra led us to a pub with a faded sign that said The Red Sky Inn.

We walked up to the counter where the innkeeper was serving food and drinks. Sierra loudly cleared her throat. "Excuse me, I'm looking for a friend of mine. His name is Julius Aurelius."

The innkeeper was of the race of men; he was bald, rather short and round, and he was wearing a white, collared shirt with an old grey vest. "Oh yeah, he said someone might come looking for him. Sorry, he's not here."

"What?" Sierra said in surprise. "Where did he go? Did he say why he left?"

"Some men arrived and said he had been summoned back to the capital city of the Kingdom of the Sun. Official business. He didn't seem too happy about it, but he went with them." The innkeeper said, scratching his head. "It was all rather odd. He had already paid me in advance for a month's rent and then suddenly left. Didn't even ask for a refund."

Sierra turned back to me and Demetri with a worried look. "He was supposed to be here when I brought you to meet him. That was the plan. He had information we need..." Before I could ask her more about it, she turned around to the innkeeper again. "How long ago did he leave?"

"Oh, it must have been about five days ago now."

Sierra bit her lip nervously, then seemed to make a decision. "Well, we'll need two rooms for the night. Do you have something private?"

I was surprised when he narrowed his eyes and leaned closer to Sierra, and his face suddenly contorted into an angry scowl. "Wait a minute! We don't serve Vampires here, so you three best leave now!"

Sierra looked shocked and didn't know what to say. She glanced back at me and I felt anger rising up in my throat.

"Excuse me, gentle innkeeper!" I said with a harsh whisper. "But I'm prince Septimus of the Kingdom of the Sky, and you have not only insulted my friend, you have insulted me! I could have you jailed and beaten for that."

The innkeeper went completely pale, and stuttered. "Oh, my apologies my prince! I didn't recognize you...the king has so many sons...I mean, if I had known it was you I would have—"

I interrupted him. "Enough with the excuses! Are you going to serve us, or do I need to call in my guards?"

"No need for that—of c-course we'll serve you here. And you won't be needing to pay! E-everything is on the house, nothing but the best service for you and your friends as long you stay! Uh, will this be a long stay?" He asked nervously.

Both Demetri and I shrugged, then we looked at Sierra because she was the one who had this whole trip planned out. Sierra looked at both of us and smiled. "Just for tonight. We leave in the morning."

The innkeeper seemed relieved. "Excellent, just staying for the night. Must have a long journey ahead of you, then?" Sierra frowned. "Mind your own business, and we will mind ours."

"Didn't mean to pry, just making conversation. Camilla!" He called over his shoulder to a mousy-haired girl who was carrying a pitcher of ale. "Put that down and go tidy up our best rooms. You'll have to move old lady Goonborg out. Put her into the room down the hall." She set down the pitcher and scurried away.

"I assume your best rooms are secure?" Sierra asked. "Nothing but the best for you—there are iron bolt locks on the doors. Here are your room keys, now go ahead and take a seat."

We took the room keys and sat down at the only free table left in the room, which was close to the front counter. The table was oddly triangular so we each had a side to sit at, Sierra was at my left and Demetri was at my right.

"Once you get the innkeeper to mind his manners, this place isn't so bad." Sierra said.

I turned to look at Sierra. "So what is this quest exactly?" I asked.

Sierra looked around the inn and it seemed that everyone else was busy in their own conversations, but she lowered her voice anyway. "We are going to kill my parents."

Demetri and I went pale. "Wow, that's really dark!"

"And a pretty ruthless way to get the throne." Demetri said.

"No, no, no! I'm not trying to gain the throne or anything selfish from this." Sierra said reassuringly.

Demetri wasn't convinced "So why are we going to..."

Just then the innkeeper came to take our orders.

"So what will you be having? I'm not interrupting something am I?" The innkeeper asked.

Demetri, Sierra, and I all looked at each other and we all replied. "No."

I looked at the menu which was written on stained parchment, and I thought for a few seconds, "I'll have a steak with fried potatoes, and some thin ale." I said. "Make it mostly water—with ice—that's the way I like it."

The innkeeper raised an eyebrow.

Demetri shrugged "I'll have what he's having." Demetri said.

Sierra looked hungry, but not for food. She was a Vampire after all. "Uh, same as them." Sierra said.

The innkeeper smiled "Okay, so three steaks, three ale-flavored waters with ice, and some fried potatoes. I'll be back with your food."

The innkeeper left and we went back to conversing. Sierra frowned. "Okay, just let me start from the beginning. So, as you probably know, the first king of the Vampires was Dalmarius the Cruel, and he sought immortal life." Sierra said.

I was already confused. "Wait, didn't he already have immortal life? You know being an Elf and all?" I asked.

Sierra chuckled. "Elves and Vampires can't die of old age or diseases, but they can be killed in battle, in accidents, by some poisons, and of course, by monsters and wild beasts. That wasn't good enough for Dalmarius the Cruel—he wanted to be completely invincible."

"Ah, I see." I replied. "He sought invincibility!"

Sierra laughed "Okay, no more interruptions! So Dalmarius sought invincible immortality and found the instruments to gain it, but never got the chance to use them because his son, Darius, was just as evil, and he ended up murdering his parents in his own jealous bid to gain power and dominate everyone else."

"Brutal." I said.

"Why are nasty people surprised when their nasty kids turn on them?" Demetri asked.

Sierra ignored him. "Anyway, this murderous prince, Darius, had been studying all kinds of dark magic, so when he became king he went to his father's evil priests and gave them a new project to work on. He instructed them how forge two golden amulets, one for him and one for his wife, that were made in such a way that they could capture ethereal matter."

"What would that do?" I asked.

"What does that even mean?" Demetri asked.

"It means it could absorb and hold spirits or souls. Their own souls, to be precise. The magic amulets were supposed to create an ethereal matrix that would house and protect their souls inside the amulets, and in return, give them full immortality."

"Did it work?" I asked.

"Not exactly. After they had the amulets made, another ambitious Vampire clan carried out a coup and assassinated them. It turned out that the magic only worked part way. It was very difficult to kill them—it took a terrible amount of power and was extremely gruesome—but when their bodies were destroyed, their souls were captured in the amulets. The new Vampire king took the throne, and at that point the amulets were considered to be cursed, so they were buried with the remains of Darius and Ursula for centuries until..."

"Sorry to interrupt, but here's your food." The innkeeper said.

The food smelled delicious, but I noticed something was missing. "Hey, where's our ice? We all just have water."

"Oh, sorry, I forgot! Here we go..." The innkeeper plucked balls of ice out of thin air and dropped a couple into each of our cups. (That probably doesn't happen where you live, but most innkeepers and tavern keepers in this part of the land are kitchen mages and can use their magic to cook food, make ice, etc, etc.)

The innkeeper smiled and went back to his counter, and once again we continued our conversation while digging into our food. (And the food was delicious).

"So, what do these amulets have to do with anything?" Demetri said through a mouthful of fried potatoes. "They didn't work and they got buried with the people they killed."

Sierra rearranged the food on her plate, but wasn't really eating anything. "Well, years later my parents came to power, and like most Vampire kings and queens, they were concerned about being assassinated by rivals. They had learned something of the old amulet lore, and set about on a search for someone who could teach them more. That eventually led them to capture a wizard from an Orc tribe who knew how to combine different kinds of magic."

"They used Orc magic?"

"No, but they were able to force the wizard to do it. My parents had the graves of King Darius and Queen Ursula dug up so they could get the amulets, then they made the captured wizard perform terrible experiments on the amulets."

"What kind of experiments?"

"I don't know exactly, but the result was a lot of dead test subjects. They experimented on their own people."

"Your parents don't sound very nice." Demetri said, and I agreed with him.

Sierra chuckled darkly. "That was nothing—they got a lot worse. They had this wizard doing all kinds of horrible things, and they promised to release him if he could make the amulets work the way they were supposed to. I think their real intention was to have the wizard killed anyway. Eventually the wizard made a breakthrough. He discovered that the souls of King Darius and Queen Ursula were still trapped in the amulets, and he found a way to harness and amplify their lust for power."

"Are you saying he was able to use the power of their trapped souls?" Demetri asked.

"It's worse than that. He essentially turned them into power magnets. As soon as the amulets were activated, their lust for power was amplified a million times, and they drained all of the powers of every Vampire in the entire world."

"Woah...are you saying that no Vampires can use their powers now?" I asked. "Aren't your parents afraid that their kingdom will be attacked by their enemies?"

Sierra chuckled, but there was no humor in her voice. "No, they're not afraid of anything. That's the whole problem—the amulets made my parents invincible, and a million times more evil."

"So they are the only Vampires with power now?" Demetri asked.

"Exactly—and they have all the power. They will never be assassinated, unlike all the rulers of the Vampires before them. Anyone who tries to attack them will be attacking all of the power of every Vampire in the world. No one can stand against them, but all of the power of the Vampires still isn't enough for my parents. They want more, and they don't care how many people will die for them to achieve complete domination of every kingdom."

"That wouldn't be good for me or my family." I said.

"Wait, I don't understand." Demetri said. "You're their daughter. Why would you want to stop your parents from doing this? It seems like you would be in a pretty good position if your parents ruled the whole world?"

"Yeah, and you already forgot what I just told you. The amulets made them invincible and totally evil. Now my parents kill people all the time—for no reason—just because they can. You can't imagine how horrible it was to live with them. You know, I didn't used to be an only child." Sierra paused for a moment and looked down at her plate. "I used to have three sisters and two brothers, before my parents killed them."

"They killed their own children??" I asked, horrified.

"Not all at once, and not on purpose, at first." Sierra wiped her eyes. "I don't like to think about what they did. The kind of power they have gained changed them into monsters."

"That sounds so terrible." I said. "How did you survive?"

"I've always been a survivor. When they absorbed all that power I learned very quickly not to make them angry. I learned how to see the signs and knew when to hide. I made sure I was out of their way when they went into a power rage. But it was only a matter of time before they turned on me, so I eventually escaped. And I came to find you, Septimus."

"Me? Why would you come looking for me?"

Sierra looked at me earnestly. "Because our quest is to destroy these amulets before my parents unleash an attack on the whole world."

Once again I was majorly confused. "You just told us your parents have absorbed all of the power of every Vampire in the world. So how exactly do you think we're going to destroy these invincible amulets? And what does this have to do with me?" I asked.

Sierra smiled, "Well, one night I snuck into their room while they were sleeping and carefully made rubbings of the runes that are on the amulets. I sent them to an old friend—Julius Aurelius—who is an expert in ancient languages. A few weeks later I received a letter saying I should meet with him as soon as possible—and that I needed to bring the seventh son of King Leon."

I raised my brow. "The runes mentioned me?" I asked.

Sierra nodded, "Yes, the runes said that we need a prince who is a seventh son of the Kingdom of the Sky."

I looked over at Demetri whose surprised expression must have reflected my own.

"And our plan was that I was to bring you here, to the Red Sky Inn, to meet Julius Aurelius. Then we would learn what he has discovered about destroying the amulets."

"But now we're going to have to meet him in the Kingdom of the Sun."

Sierra frowned. "That's right, and it's getting late. Don't stay up too late thinking about all of this because we need to leave first thing in the morning. I'm off to bed." Sierra said, and grabbed her bag and went up to her room.

Demetri and I were stunned, not sure what to say, so we went back to eating. We noticed the noise level in the room was rising as the people had more to drink. It was raucous singing and laughing now, but it would probably turn into a fight before long. It wouldn't be a good idea to get caught up in anything like that, so Demetri finished our meals, then grabbed our bags and took them to our rooms.

Demetri and I shared a room at the top of the second landing that was across the hall from Sierra's. I unlocked the door and dropped my bag on the floor next to one of the beds—thank goodness there were two beds or one of us would have had to sleep on the floor!

I sat on my bed for a moment, but something was troubling me, and not just the fact that Sierra's parents had killed her siblings, or that the most evil objects in the world practically had my name written on them. "Demetri, did you notice how little Sierra ate?" I asked.

Demetri was pulling his nightshirt out of his bag.

"Yeah, sort of. Maybe she's trying to stay skinny."

I thought for a minute then I had an idea. "Of course, she's a Vampire! I'll be right back—I'm going to go get some blood for Sierra." I said.

"Where are you going to get blood?" Demetri asked.

"We had steak didn't we? I'll just ask the innkeeper for a cup of blood from the cow." I said.

"Why exactly?" Demetri asked.

"We can't have the navigator of our company dying of hunger." I said.

"Okay, have fun! I'm going to change and go to sleep, good night!" Demetri said.

"Night!" I said.

I left and went to the innkeeper who was still at his counter looking like he was about to go to his room.

"Excuse me, innkeeper, uh...I need another drink."

"More ice water?"

"No, I was wondering if you have a cup of cow blood?" I asked.

The innkeeper looked shocked, but then understanding crossed his face. "The blood is for the Vampire girl, right?"

"Why do you have such a hard time minding your own business?"

"I'm sorry, I'm sorry! Okay, here I always drain raw meat of its blood to give it to a warlock who lives in the forest…for his potions, obviously." The innkeeper said.

He handed me the cup which I took to Sierra's door. I knocked thrice and whispered, "Sierra it's me, Septimus! I got you something."

Sierra opened the door and she was wearing a silver nightgown with sapphire robe. "Yeah?"

"Um, I noticed that you didn't eat much so I got you some blood." I handed her the cup of cow blood and I swear it sparkled in the candlelight. Sierra took it looked at it for a couple seconds then looked back up at me.

"Whose blood is this?" Sierra asked.

"Demetri's." I said. "Nah, just kidding! That blood came from the same cow our steak did."

"Oh, good." She chuckled. "Thank you Septimus. I was afraid this came from a person, which is forbidden among civilized Vampires. We only drink the blood of animals, not sentient beings."

"I'm glad to hear that. Well...it's late...see you tomorrow...goodnight." I said.

"Night Septimus." Sierra said.

I went back to my room, changed into my nightshirt, and fell asleep faster than I expected.

Chapter Five: An Early Start

I was woken up by Demetri who had a terrified look on his face.

I yawned. "What is it Demetri?"

Demetri stuttered. "He's here! Victor is here!"

I sprang up out of my bed. "What!? He's like, in the inn?"

"No, no he's outside—I saw him out the window heading for the stables, and I heard him asking about you."

We hadn't seen him on the road, but he must have tracked us here. "We need to leave. Hurry and get dressed and pack up. I'll go tell Sierra."

We quickly pulled off our nightshirts and put on our travel clothes. I opened the door to our room and peeked outside, then slipped across the hall and knocked on Sierra's door.

"Sierra, wake up! We need to leave, now. Get dressed and pack your things!" I whispered as loud as I dared. It was just getting light outside and still pretty quiet, which meant that most people were still sleeping.

I went back into my room and pulled on my boots, grabbed my bag, and I made sure to fasten my sword to my belt. "Hey Demetri, I hope you're ready to use your sword."

Demetri quickly got his sword and fastened it to his belt. "Readier than you are! But I think we're going to be in trouble if it comes to that."

"Yeah," I sighed. "There are a lot more of them than there are of us. Hopefully we can get out of here without being seen."

We put pillows under our blankets, just in case they checked there, then quietly closed and locked our door. When I knocked on Sierra's door again, she opened it almost immediately, and was wearing her dusty travel clothes and a dagger on her belt.

Sierra looked nervous. "You sounded scared. What's this all about?"

"Victor is here, and he knows I'm in town."

"Yeah, we've got to go now!" Demetri added.

We pulled up the hoods on our cloaks to hide our faces and quickly made our way down the stairs to the front counter. It was unattended, so we left our keys on the counter and headed for the door. There were a few people sitting at tables eating breakfast who glanced up at us as we passed. We were hurrying so fast that we almost ran into the innkeeper's daughter, Camilla, who was carrying two plates of food.

"Sorry," I mumbled.

"Are you leaving so soon?" She asked. "You haven't had breakfast."

We didn't answer her because we were already opening the door...when we saw Victor! He and a few of his thugs were approaching the inn, and they were being led by one of the stable boys who was pointing at the door. We quickly shut the door and went to the far side of the room, to a table partially obscured by a wooden archway.

"Yes, we'll have breakfast after all," I called to Camilla.

"Bacon and hash browns, please."

"And orange juice." Demetri said.

"And red juice!" Sierra said.

This table was rectangular, unlike our table last night. All three of us sat on the side closest to the wall so we were hidden in the shadows but could clearly see the front door. I sat in the middle and once again Demetri sat on my right and Sierra sat on my left. There was a book on the table which Demetri immediately picked up. He covered his face with it to make it appear that he was reading.

Sierra and I both looked panicked at Demetri. "It's dim over here, but if they come close, how will Sierra and I cover our faces?"

"Sounds like your problem." Demetri said.

"If we get caught, you get caught too!" I whispered harshly.

Demetri looked at us from behind his book and whispered. "Okay, I have an idea. Kiss her! That will cover both your faces!"

My face felt hot with embarrassment. "I'm not going to kiss her!" I whispered quickly, because we could hear boots stomping up the wooden steps to the inn. "She drank blood last night...and I wouldn't kiss her even if she didn't drink blood last night! Give me the book and you kiss her!"

Demetri looked at me with a serious face, and whispered. "Septimus, you have to kiss her or we are all dead!" Then he shoved his face back into his book and pretended to read.

Just then the door burst open, and Victor and his men walked into the inn. The innkeeper came from the kitchen at that moment and greeted them, but I could see Victor's men squinting around at the people in the dim light. I felt panic rush over me and quickly made a decision.

I looked at Demetri and took a deep breath, and whispered "Fine! I'll do it!"

Demetri looked at Sierra for confirmation "Fine I guess I'm being forced into this as well." She shrugged.

I scooched my chair closer to Sierra's. I wrapped my arms around her and then she kissed me, and I kissed her, and—plot twist—we were both kissing. With our hoods up, the kiss completely covered our faces. I felt a little disgust for a couple of seconds, but then Victor's growling voice caught my attention.

"Listen to me, you wee man, I'm for looking Septimus Legion!" Victor said. "I heard he was staying here, and we would like to pay him a visit, so I'll be needing the key to his room if you'll be so kind."

The innkeeper sounded frightened. "I'm sorry, but I cannot give out keys to guest rooms while people are still sleeping. Besides, I don't recall having a guest by the name of Legion. I'm sure you understand."

"Oh, we understand just fine, wee man…Terry, jog his memory!"

Terry was one of Victor's henchmen, who had a deep, smooth voice. "It would be my pleasure, sir!"

We heard Terry throwing some punches and the innkeeper gasping in pain. We also heard the customers sitting at the tables gasping and whispering.

"That's enough, Terry. I'll wager this wee man is beginning to remember a guest named Septimus Legion who arrived last night." Victor said.

We heard Terry stop punching, and the innkeeper was groaning in pain. "Leave me alone...they're in rooms 7 and 8. Here, take the keys!" He gasped.

"Pleasure doing business with you!" Victor said.

We heard Victor and his men stomp up the stairs toward our rooms. We waited a few seconds longer then jumped up from our seats and raced out the front door. We ran straight toward the stables, but as we approached we saw that one of Victor's henchmen was waiting there. He saw my face and there was a flash of recognition in his eyes, so we quickly turned around to run the other direction...and ran right into another group of henchmen who grabbed us by the shoulders.

One of the henchmen spoke in a whiny, high-pitched voice, "Victor will be wanting to see you! Let's just wait here at the stables for him. Malkus, go tell Victor we got them and don't worry, we'll hold onto them till you get back with the master."

Malkus looked the least educated of the four henchmen holding us. "Alrighty! I'll be getting the master now."

We struggled, but it was useless. We were outnumbered, and after a couple of punches to the gut Demetri and I felt like the innkeeper did, and weren't interested in resisting anymore. Malkus returned a minute later with Victor and his other two henchmen.

Victor grinned victoriously and I saw his yellowed teeth. Like the innkeeper and some of the townspeople, Victor was of the race of men, though clearly not the most handsome specimen. Victor was about the same height as Sierra, Demetri, and me, but he was bald and had dirty stubble on his face. He wore some pieces of leather armor over a dirty white shirt that was tucked into stained brown pants, and wore a dusty pair of black boots. He had no helmet, but his scarred head was probably protection enough.

"Well, well, well...allo there Septimus! Here you are, right where I thought you would be, looking a little shabbier than I remembered. And this time you're here without your father's protection."

I was still breathing hard from being punched in the gut, but I forced a smile. "Greetings Victor, you're even uglier than I remembered, and I have all the protection I need."

Victor laughed. "Who? Your little friend Demetri? He wouldn't even be able to protect you from a wee wolf cub."

Then Victor noticed Sierra. "Well, hello, lassie! Was that you and Septimus I saw kissing in the inn?" Victor looked right at Sierra. "You must be very important to Septimus, or the other way around!"

Victor looked at his men, and then put his hand on Sierra's shoulder. "Demetri isn't worth much, but Septimus should fetch a pretty ransom. I have something else in mind for the girl...I'll bet she could give me a wee little kiss, too!" Victor and his men started laughing hysterically.

I could feel my face and my ears burning with anger, but before I could do anything Sierra kicked Victor in the crotch so hard that he was lifted off the ground and then fell in a heap. Suddenly there was chaos all around.

I wrenched my hands free and elbowed my captor in the nose. Someone was shouting in pain behind me as I fumbled for my sword. I glanced over my shoulder and saw that Demetri had back-kicked the henchman holding him. The man was now on the ground yelling, while others were shouting and rushing toward me. I was too slow. Someone punched me hard in the side, and a strong hand stopped me from unsheathing my weapon.

Demetri fared much better. In a flash he had unsheathed his sword and swung at Victor, who was struggling to his feet and limping sorely from his encounter with Sierra's foot. But Victor was still quick enough to dodge out of the way just in time. He might be older and moving uncomfortably, but he was a much more accomplished swordsman than Demetri. He gritted his teeth in a fierce grin as he ripped his sword from its sheath with a flourish.

Demetri looked a little uncertain, but then he lunged forward and attacked again. Victor hopped out of the way, and then swung back so viciously that I thought Demetri was done for. But Demetri raised his sword just in time and parried the blow with a loud clang that startled Victor and rattled his sword arm.

Victor stepped back astonished. He must have underestimated Demetri's strength—not accounting for the thick arms that were developed through hours of beating a hammer against hot iron at the forge.

Demetri spun around and slashed threateningly in the air to discourage a couple of the henchmen who looked like they were thinking of stepping in to help Victor. They stayed back as Victor and Demetri circled each other and then sprang forward with a clash of metal.

Meanwhile, both Sierra and I were struggling uselessly against several other thugs. We had each been caught by a couple of strong henchmen before we could draw our swords.

Now both of us were being crushed by men who pinned our arms to our sides, while another hit and slapped us in the face until we stopped kicking and fighting. Our fight was over almost as soon as it had begun.

All we could do was watch helplessly as Demetri fought Victor. He went in for another attack and Victor once again blocked expertly, then slashed his sword toward Demetri who blocked again with a jarringly powerful clash.

This went on for almost a minute with one of them swinging left, right, up, and down and then having the other block the attack with a clang of swords. Soon, both of them were huffing and sweating, and it was only a matter of time before one of them reacted too slowly or made a mistake.

Curious townspeople were starting to gather around at a cautious distance to watch the fight. They were being treated to some morning entertainment.

Victor glared at Demetri as they continued to wheeze and spit as they circled around each other. Suddenly Victor lunged at Demetri, who seemed to have been taken by surprise. Demetri stumbled out of the way of Victor's sword, and threw out a hand to catch his fall as he almost went to the ground. Victor stepped past him, then spun and charged toward him again. At that moment, Demetri jerked up straight and hurled a handful of dirt and pebbles he had just picked up from the ground, pelting Victor in the face.

Victor screamed in anger and blindly swung his sword, but now Demetri easily dodged the blow and slashed his blade down on Victor's sword arm. Victor screamed in pain and dropped his sword.

A red stain began to spread across his dirty white sleeve. He clutched the wound as blood began rushing out of the deep cut, barely aware that Demetri was now behind him, gripping the back of his sweaty neck and holding his blade to his throat.

Demetri was still breathing heavily, but he grinned triumphantly at the townspeople who were now coming out in greater numbers to see what the commotion was about.

"Well, Victor!" Demetri said, after he caught his breath. "Would you look at this? We have a great crowd of witnesses here to see how you and your cowardly henchmen treat the royalty of the Kingdom of the Sky. Attacking three young people with a whole pack of thugs? That's just bad sportsmanship."

Grumbling and boos erupted from the crowd.

Demetri grinned and then continued, speaking directly to his audience. "Fine people of Wesst, I apologize for disrupting your quiet morning. The least I can do is offer you some entertainment! Who would like to see me take the rascal's head off right now?"

There were a few raucous cheers as well as a few gasps.

Victor had turned pale as a sheet. "No...let me live and we'll let you go...we'll leave you alone!" Victor choked. "I promise."

"Terry, did you hear that?"

Terry blinked at him in stunned disbelief.

"Come on now, Terry. Don't make him say it again..."

"I heard 'im." Terry said, but he was still holding Sierra tightly and not letting go.

"Then you have a decision to make. Either you, Malkus, Butt-face, Armpit-breath, and all the other vermin are going to let go of Septimus and Sierra and let us be on our way, or…" he paused for effect, and I could tell he was really enjoying this. "Or I can relieve Victor of his ugly head and we can have a nice game of kickball here in the street to entertain the people of Wesst. What's it going to be?"

Terry swore under his breath, then grudgingly let go of Sierra. The other henchmen released me, too, but Demetri was still holding the blade to Victor's throat.

"And now you're all going to walk away, and if I see any of you following us, it will be your head I'll go after next. You understand?"

Terry grunted, and Demetri lowered his blade, but gave Victor a shove that sent him sprawling in the dirt.

There were jeers and laughs from the crowd as Victor slowly arose and then slunk away toward the inn, clutching his bloody arm and surrounded by his sulking henchmen. We had no reason to linger, so we quickly got our horses out of the stables and strapped down our bags. Then we mounted and rode off, following Sierra to our next destination, the Kingdom of the Sun.

Chapter Six: The Battle for Men

A week after our conflict with Victor we were setting up our campsite again, as we had every night since we left the town of Wesst. Instead of following the main road we had gone north, fording the Fielign River and traveling deep into the Dark Forest. We had now reached the Western edge of the forest and pitched our tents in a field in the shadow of the trees. There we built a fire and were finally cooking some venison after days of eating small game.

Demetri, Sierra, and I had been hunting every morning, tracking deer along the deer paths in the forest and taking a shot at one whenever we got close enough. We had seen a deer nearly every day, but we had wasted a lot of arrows because none of us was very good with a bow.

It was too bad my cousin, Olivia, wasn't with us because she was the best archer I had ever known. Two days ago Sierra hit a deer close to the heart, but she hadn't had time to draw the bow all the way back, and the arrow barely penetrated the hide. The deer bolted and the arrow fell out on the ground. We wasted a few more arrows during the chase, but we couldn't keep up with that deer and lost its trail.

Today Demetri and I had been lucky—or so we thought at first. We finally tracked down a deer and brought it down with a lucky shot (or 3 lucky arrows and 5 unlucky ones, to be completely honest), so instead of just rabbits or squirrels for the morning stew, we would have real meat for days! But this turned out to be a lot more work than I expected.

After putting three arrows into the deer we had to chase it on foot for nearly a mile before it finally fell dead. We cleaned and dressed the carcass on the spot, filling a canteen with blood for Sierra, then cut it into quarters and hung it from a tree. That was just the beginning.

We were hot and sticky with sweat and covered with blood, so we had to find a stream to rinse off in. When we got back to camp Sierra was angry with us for taking so long (until I gave her the canteen full of fresh blood). She had already packed up the entire camp herself and loaded our horses. But then it took two hours for us to lead our horses through the thick forest and find our way back to where we had left the meat.

When we finally found it, there was an eagle and a bunch of ravens picking at the pile of entrails on the ground, but thankfully no other scavengers. The last thing we wanted to see was a pack of wolves or a bear that had smelled our prey.

We quickly took the hanging meat down from the tree, divided it into three bundles wrapped in cloth, and loaded it onto the backs of each of our horses. We walked our horses until we found another deer trail that led in roughly the right direction (according to Sierra), and continued our journey through the forest. By that time it was already early afternoon and the hunt had taken up a good part of the day. We travelled through the forest the rest of the day, and came to the edge of the forested hills in the dying light of the evening.

Now it was completely dark and we were sitting around the fire, tired but happy, enjoying the smell of venison roasting on a spit. I decided it was time to tease Sierra again. "So Sierra, how much longer until we get to…the Kingdom of the Sun? That's where we are going, right?"

Sierra sighed. "Septimus, you have already asked me this thirteen times today! As I have informed you we should get there tomorrow-ish. But yes we are going to the Kingdom of the Sun."

Demetri chuckled in relief. "Oh good, we just need to make it one more day!"

"I said tomorrow-*ish*. It might be two days, especially now that our horses are loaded down with extra weight."

"And you're sure we're on the right path?" I asked.

"Are you seriously doubting my judgement? We've gone the straightest way. So far we've avoided people like Victor who ambush unprotected travelers on the roads."

"I wasn't doubting you, I was just…"

Sierra glared at me, and I couldn't think of anything to say so I just shrugged my shoulders.

Sierra rolled her eyes and then shivered. "It's cold, I'm going to get my blanket from my tent." Sierra got up and went into her tent.

Demetri looked confused. "Okay, sounds good. Septimus and I will just sit here by the *WARM* fire."

She made a rude gesture and Demetri laughed.

After she disappeared into her tent he looked puzzled. "Why did she do that?"

I had no idea. Girls were such a mystery. "Vampires must get cold easily." I said lamely.

Demetri laughed. "Oh so now you're an expert on Vampires?" Then he furrowed his brow. "So, uh, anyways Septimus, I didn't get to ask earlier, but how was it? Was it cold?"

"How was what?" I knew exactly what he was talking about, but I pretended to be confused.

Demetri sighed. "Your kiss with Sierra, obviously!"

"Hmm, I forgot about that," I lied. I had thought about it a hundred times since then, even though it made me uncomfortable. I thought about it when I was riding beside her, when we were hunting together in the forest, and when we made camp and sat around the fire at night. I thought about it when I laid awake on my back in my tent, trying to go to sleep. I didn't think I had any feelings for her before that stupid kiss, but now her face kept popping up in my mind at odd times.

"Come on, man! Was it gross? Did she bite your lip? Do you think you might turn into a Vampire now?"

I laughed. "No, she didn't draw blood, and, well I mean...it wasn't bad. But ehh, I mean, she is a Vampire after all..."

"You don't like her?" He asked, and I noticed something strange about his constricted tone.

"Why do you care?" I thought for a second. "Oh! You like Sierra, don't you?"

Demetri's face turned as red as a rose. "Um…no, no I don't."

I was stunned. "Holy catfish! You like her, don't you!?" Sierra's tent flap flew open and she emerged, wrapped in a blanket. "What is this about catfish?"

"Nothing! You wouldn't understand." Demetri answered quickly.

"Why wouldn't I understand?" Sierra asked.

"What Demetri means is that we were just talking about...guy stuff." I said.

Sierra chuckled as she sat down. "Guy stuff. You mean like burps and farts and foot fungus?" She didn't wait for a response. "So, is the meat about done cooking?"

I stood up trying not to laugh, wondering how much Sierra had heard, and then felt myself blushing, too. What was wrong with me? Sierra was just a friend.

I busied myself with one of Demetri's cooking knives and cut off a piece of the venison. It was hot and greasy and I burnt my fingers a little, but I took a small bite and looked at the inside. "It's cooked all the way through." I said. "And it tastes really good!"

The conversation around the fire was a little awkward that night, but we ate, cleaned up our meal, put out the fire, and went right to sleep. We were all exhausted and anxious to get up at first light to continue our journey—and hopefully arrive at the Kingdom of the Sun the next day.

I awoke to the distant sound of clanging metal, yelling, and loud crashes which shook the ground. I leapt up and peaked out of my tent. Somehow it was already light. How had we overslept? Then I noticed in the distance, across the field and further down the valley, that there was a battle taking place.

It had been dark when we arrived the night before, and we hadn't seen any campfires. I guessed that the two armies must have been marching during the night and clashed here this morning. Maybe they had been concealed by magic, who knows? From what I could see it was a battle between Orcs and Men, and it was beginning to grow very fierce.

I saw that the men had formed their ranks in front of the trees that lined the river, and they were being assaulted by a larger army of Orcs that seemed to have taken them by surprise. Now trees were getting knocked to the ground by Orc catapults and there were fires erupting amid the combatants on both sides. Magic was being deployed by both Orcs and Men, and in places the ground and grass was exploding, leaving craters in the earth.

In a moment Demetri and Sierra were up and we were quickly taking down camp.
Sierra looked worried. "We have to go before we get caught up in that battle."

I looked towards the battle again. "Which way is it to the Kingdom of the Sun?"

Sierra scowled. "Straight through that battle."

"Well, then we'll just have to go around." Demetri said.

Sierra shook her head. "There is no place to cross the river for miles, and the mountains rise pretty steeply to the North. Maybe we should just wait until the battle is over and continue after they leave?"

I had another idea. "You think? Or maybe we should go help them."

"Help who? The Orcs?" Demetri questioned sarcastically. We were far behind the Orc lines, and the armies of Men were on the other side of the battle.

I sighed, "Obviously not the Orcs. Why would you even say that, you're half Man!"

"That's my back half. My front half is all Elf." Demetri grinned.

"Well, you need to get up off your Man-half and look for an opportunity to help the knights of Men. We're all outsiders here, but by joining the fight we might be able to win their welcome to the Kingdom of the Sun. That's where we're headed anyway. That's where Sierra's scholar friend is."

Sierra thought for a moment. "That could possibly work, if we were careful...and if we found the right opportunity."

Demetri raised his eyebrow. "My family decided not to live in the Kingdom of the Sun because the armies of Men were always going to war. Sure, that could work, Sierra. That could work to get us killed!"

Demetri wasn't wrong, but I forced a chuckle. "Demetri, you've been telling me you wanted to be in a real battle ever since we were little. You resented your father for taking you away from the Kingdom of the Sun. Are you going to turn down the chance at glory now?"

Demetri looked at the battle with apprehension, but then took a deep breath and gritted his teeth. "Fine, at least if I die, I'll die a hero."

I wasn't feeling very confident, but I managed to smile. "That's the spirit! Except let's try not to die, okay?"

As we finished packing up, I realized that this was crazy. We had used the last of our arrows on yesterday's deer hunt. Demetri was the best with a sword, but that wasn't saying much. None of us had any armor, and none of us had been trained as soldiers or had any experience fighting on horseback.

I had never actually seen an Orc up close, but I had heard that they were terrifying monsters with pale, blotchy skin, sharp teeth and claws, black armor, and vicious blades. As far as I knew, they had never been known to show mercy to a Man or an Elf. In fact, I was shaking as I quickly dressed and fastened my sword to my belt.

But none of us wanted to appear afraid, so Demetri gave Sierra his spare sword for her to use instead of her dagger, then we mounted up and did something completely crazy. We rode toward the battle.

My heart seemed to be pounding as loud as our horses' hooves as we galloped toward the fighting. Our camping gear and the deer meat clanged and bounced behind our saddles. Explosions were still erupting in front of us, and the howls and screams of the fighting and dying enemies sent chills down my spine.

"What are we doing?" Demetri shouted.

I realized he was asking me what the plan was. As usual, I didn't really have a plan. I looked around for the leaders of the Knights of Men and decided to cut through the Orc lines toward them.

"Sierra, you take the left!" I shouted, not certain that she could even hear me over the pounding of hooves and the sounds of battle. "Demetri, you take the right. I'm going to cut right down the center." I glanced at both of them, and then drew my sword.

"Attack!" I shouted, and my voice cracked. But thankfully they both drew their swords in response.

We raced into the noisy battle and burst through the back of the Orc lines, screaming and swinging our swords wildly at any Orc within reach. We cut through their ranks, more because of the speed and weight of our horses, with our blades banging against helmets and bouncing off Orc armor as we went. We had no experience at this and weren't doing much damage to the snarling enemy.

Orc scimitars and axes chopped at us as we thundered through their lines, but our clunky camping gear and bundles of deer meat took the brunt of their blows. At some point everything fell off the back of my horse, causing the Orcs who had begun pursuing me to trip and stumble over it, but I just kept riding and banging my sword on anything I could reach.

I probably didn't give a serious wound to a single Orc, let alone kill anyone. However, the three of us had taken the Orcs by surprise and created some confusion. Some of the Orcs thought they were being attacked from behind by reinforcements for the armies of Men, and that slowed the advance of part of the Orc line. Many of the Orcs actually halted and turned around to face us. This was just what the Men needed.

Before we had arrived the Orcs seemed to have been gaining the upper hand, pushing the Men back toward the river. But now we had accidentally created a diversion, and the Men were taking advantage of it and pressing forward into a gap in the Orc line.

My horse started to slow as I approached the front of the Orc line, and now I could see, hear, and smell the results of the real battle. There was no glory here. There were dead and dying Orcs and Men, screaming in fear and pain as swords chopped and clanged, axes beat on shields, and explosions erupted around them. The air was filled with a horrible stench like an open sewer. The ground was smeared with both the red blood of Men and Orc blood that was as black as oil, slippery under my horse's hooves.

I couldn't see Sierra or Demetri and my head was spinning. I barely dodged a boulder from one of the Orc catapults that crashed into the wall of shields of the Men in front of me, but I fell off my horse and dropped my sword.

I was instantly covered in the horrible gore of the battlefield. That might have saved me, because after my horse ran away, the Orcs charged past me and ignored me. I saw the Knights of Men using their power of light against the Orc warriors, which scorched their skin and left black wounds that oozed oily blood. The Orcs used their dark magic to make a blade of night which could cut through swords, shields, and thick armor of the Men, tearing unfortunate warriors asunder.

Then I noticed an Orc riding through the ranks on a giant wolf, toward the gap that had been blasted through the wall of Men's shields. He appeared to be the leader of the Orc army, and I could see his target was the general of the army of Men, who was charging forward on foot to block the gap.

I fumbled for my sword and gripped the hilt, slashing my blade at the wolf's hind leg as it passed. It howled in pain and turned to bite me. But just then the general stepped in front of me—laughing—and thrust his sword up through the roof of its mouth.

The wolf fell lifeless as the general pulled his sword free. The Orc Leader roared as he tumbled off the wolf's back, but he landed on his feet again. He was furious and lashed out with a dark blast of magic that met a white blast of magic from the general. Sparks and smoke erupted around them, but their magic was evenly matched and neither could gain the upper hand.

The Orc roared again and swung his great scimitar, which collided with the general's sword in a jarring clang. The Orc formed a dark blade with his other hand, but before he could slash with it, the general gripped his wrist. Smoke began rising from the Orc's wrist as the general used light magic to burn the exposed flesh.

I suddenly felt a rush of courage and leapt to my feet, gripping my sword tightly with both hands. I chopped downward with all my might, and was sprayed by black blood as I severed the Orc's hand.

The general laughed again as he threw the Orc's hand in his face, and then quickly thrust his sword through the Orc's heart. The Orc's face twisted through a variety of expressions of shock, anger, pain, and then relaxed as he fell dead.

The general freed his sword and he nodded a brief thanks to me, then ran back into action and engaged another Orc foe. I wanted to help, but my legs felt weak and I was overcome by the nightmarish sights and sounds and the horrible smell. I felt an uncontrollable urge to vomit.

I must have passed out, because I opened my eyes and realized I was back on the ground, but now I was behind the battle line of the army of Men. They were chasing the remaining Orcs, who were retreating to the forested hills we had come from the night before. The Orc catapults were in smoking ruins, and there were pale Orc corpses stained with black blood all across the field.

The smell was still awful and there was moaning all around, but now there were healers rushing to help the fallen warriors. I checked to make sure that I wasn't seriously wounded, then staggered to my feet to go and find my friends.

It was a great relief to learn that both Sierra and Demetri were alive and unharmed. They had apparently found an easier path to ride through the Orc lines to get to safety.

I told Demetri I had probably killed about twenty Orcs all together—or twenty and a half because if you think about it—I kind of half killed the Orc leader when I cut off his hand. In reality I'm pretty sure I didn't even seriously wound anyone except the Orc leader, but Demetri didn't need to know that.

In any case, the Orc army had been routed and scattered, and the remnants of the Orc army were being hunted and pursued as they retreated back to their own lands. Flocks of ravens and vultures were now circling and swooping down onto the field to peck at the corpses, and the healers were shooing them away from the wounded.

We searched for my horse, which had thankfully escaped harm in the battle, but had run far up the road away from the battlefield, and was hiding among the trees near the river. I splashed in the water to wash off the filth of battle, then it took a long time to coax my horse back to the road and calm him enough that I could ride again.

When we approached the camp of the knights of Men, they were laughing and singing drunken songs, celebrating their victory. They recognized us and cheered us as well. They motioned for us to tie our horses next to the other horses of the lieutenants and the general, and a knight approached us and smiled warmly.

"Hello friends! That was either the bravest or the most foolish ride I've ever seen through an Orc army. But either way, I'm glad you did it! I'm Lieutenant Barkis, the general…or rather, our prince, would like to meet you."

"Oh, your general that I fought with in the battle is your prince?" I asked.

"Yes indeed Sir, follow me—I shall take you to his tent."

We followed the lieutenant across camp to the general's Tent. The general's tent was huge and it even had the kingdom's flag at the top. We followed the lieutenant into the tent and he conversed with the general…prince…person…(you know what I mean).

"Prince Lokir, I have brought you our new allies." Lieutenant Barkis said.

The prince looked exactly how human princes are described in the storybooks. He had short blonde hair, bright blue eyes, chiseled features…I mean, definitely what a princess (or town girl) would go crazy for.

Prince Lokir smiled. "Greetings! We owe you our thanks." Then he looked directly at me. "Ah, you must be Septimus Legion, prince of the Kingdom of the Sky, and the one who saved my life."

I smiled back. "Yes, I am Prince Septimus, and I'm not sure I saved your life, but I was happy to help! It's rare to meet a fellow royal blood." I turn to look at Sierra. "And speaking of royal blood, this is Sierra Evans, princess of the Kingdom of the Moon."

Prince Lokir went pale for a couple seconds, then licked his lips. "She's the Vampire princess?"

I nodded my head. "Yes she is, and she, too, came to your aid today. She is perfectly harmless, as is my best friend, Demetri."

"I'm not that harmless." Demetri mumbled.

Prince Lokir went back to smiling. "Well, then you are all welcome! We would like to honor you by inviting you to the capital city of our kingdom to offer you our thanks!"

"Well we were headed there anyways, so why not?" I grinned. Joining the battle had worked out better than any of us expected.

"Very good." Lokir said. "We shall pack up camp and leave for the Kingdom of the Sun in the morning."

Chapter Seven: The Kingdom of the Sun and the Royal Ball

I was sore the next morning. I only had a few bruises from the battle with the Orcs, but my bones ached, and I couldn't forget the images, sounds, and smells that were burned into my mind. I never wanted to be in another battle again. But then I got up and saw Sierra by the fire, and the battle horrors evaporated from my mind.

We were happy to share breakfast with our new friends (Sierra drank her red juice from the canteen), and then we mounted up and rode to the Kingdom of the Sun with the army of Men. The journey took two days because we could only travel as fast as the slowest in our group, and we made many stops along the way.

We were able to see the city from a long distance away, but it wasn't until we arrived that we appreciated the enormous size of the wall surrounding the castle. Because of the recent threat of the Orcs, there were thousands of soldiers all around the high wall outside of the city. Since we were with Prince Lokir, we passed all of the guards and were waved through the gates to a waiting crowd that broke out into a cheer as we entered.

They were clapping and cheering for the armies of Men that had won the great battle against the Orcs, (and of course it was also for us because they might not have done it without our help, obviously). We waved as we rode through the streets that were lined with people, feeling quite proud of ourselves being the heroes and objects of adoration that we were. But then I noticed how many of the people were women, and that their attention was focused on Prince Lokir, and he was loving it.

Eventually we came to the stables where the parade ended, and we left our horses there and continued on foot up to the castle. This was difficult since there were dozens of admiring women who were clamoring for Lokir's attention, and they followed us until Lokir promised them invitations to the palace, and the soldiers at the first gate shooed them away. We walked up a ramp, passing through several gates, and then we were admitted into the castle where Prince Lokir took us aside before we continued to the throne room to meet the king.

Prince Lokir looked a little troubled. "Okay guys, that was the fun part, but this might be a little awkward. So here's the thing...we best not be letting my father know that Sierra's the princess of the Vampires, or he will most likely have her executed."

Sierra went pale. "Well that's reassuring."

Lokir smiled nervously. "Yeah, my father has a thing about Vampires. Bad memories or something—and some say he is going insane—but we probably shouldn't mention that, either. Any questions?"

I had a few...like why were there so many guards in this castle? And why were all the women of this city so interested in Prince Lokir? And why were we going to see a Vampire-hating king whose own son suspected was going insane?

But before I could say anything Lokir flashed a grin and said, "No questions? Great! Well let's not keep him waiting. He doesn't like that, either."

We reluctantly followed Lokir through the great doors that led into the throne room. At the far end of the hall we found Lokir's father, King Helios III, sitting on his ornate, golden throne that had an enormous gold symbol of the sun above the king's head.

The king himself didn't appear insane. He had brown eyes and short black hair, peppered with grey, and a long beard that was almost completely grey. He was pretty tall for a Man, but not Elvish-tall (like me, Sierra, and Demetri). He was wearing lavish, golden robes and a fine red shirt with golden buttons, and black trousers. The sun symbolism was everywhere, including his crown, which was in the literal shape of the sun, and was made of solid gold with emeralds and rubies encrusted into it.

King Helios stood, smiled, and motioned for us to approach. He threw out his arms and gathered Lokir in a big hug, and laughed as he slapped him on the back. "Welcome home, my son! I heard that you were ambushed?"

"It was an army of Orcs come to raid our lands—they were from the Lashgut Clan." Lokir said. "They took us by surprise this morning."

"But you gave those wretched Orcs a nasty beating at the riverside on the plain, didn't you!" The king laughed. "That must have made your morning!"

"It was quite enjoyable. You know that the only thing I like better than fighting Orcs is cavorting with women!" Lokir laughed, and his father slapped him even harder on the back and laughed louder.

Then the king released his son and looked at us. "And who are these three that you have brought before me?"

Lokir smiled. "These are our new allies, Father. They came to our aid and created a valiant diversion when the Orcs were about to overwhelm us." Taking Sierra by the hand and walking her up to the king, Lokir said: "This is Sierra Evans, a...an Elf of the Kingdom of the Sky." The king took her hand and kissed it.

Next Lokir presented Demetri. "This is Demetri Smith, a half-Elven blacksmith of the Kingdom of the Sky." The king grinned as he gripped Demetri's hand and slapped him on the shoulder.

Finally, Lokir presented me. "And this is Prince Septimus Legion of the Kingdom of the Sky, who not only came to our aid, but very likely saved my life during the battle."

I was surprised when the king grabbed my hand and pulled me in for a hug, slapping me heartily on the back before releasing me.

"I thank you for helping my soldiers defend the sacred borders of this kingdom! I thank you for saving the life of my son, Prince Lokir! I honor you for bringing peace to the Men of my kingdom by waging war on the evil Orcs that tried to defile it!"

The king paused with a huge grin on his face. Sierra, Demetri, and I smiled and nodded, but there was an awkward silence for a moment. One of the king's advisors loudly cleared his throat, and then the king continued.

"We are in your debt, Septimus Legion, of the Kingdom of the Sky! We shall inform your father that he now has a new ally! I decree that from this day forth, the kingdoms of the Sun and the Sky shall be allies, until all kingdoms are brought to ruin at the end of the world!"

Again, he paused with a great grin on his face, staring directly at us, and we were unsure what to do. This time Lokir patted his father on the arm, which seemed to prompt his father to continue.

"And now it's time to celebrate! We are going to have a Royal Ball tonight, and you three are invited!"

I smiled nervously. "You honor us greatly, King Helios. I'm certain that a Royal Ball of the Kingdom of the Sun would be an unrivaled spectacle. But, you see, we're on a very important quest, so we actually can't stay for the party."

King Helios frowned. "Come now, this is what allies do! It's just one night, and it will be one you will never forget. For the sake of the new alliance between our kingdoms, you can certainly spare to take a tiny break from your quest, can't you?" With his brow furrowed, his complexion suddenly darkened, and he looked rather fearsome.

The king's advisors had alarmed looks on their faces, so I looked at Demetri and Sierra who shrugged at me. "Okay, I guess we could stay the night and attend the Royal Ball."

King Helios smiled, his whole face brightening again, and his advisors breathed a sigh of relief. "Wonderful! I'll have Lokir show you to your rooms for the night, and my servants will prepare splendid clothes for you, for the Royal Ball."

Lokir led us from the hall to a guest wing where, once again I was sharing a room with Demetri, and Sierra got her own room. "Relax and enjoy the comforts of the palace," Lokir said. "I made a promise to invite a few ladies to the palace and I intend to keep it! I shall see you all tonight."

He left us and we entered our rooms and shut the doors, and we found that the rooms were amazing. They were decorated in lavish gold with tapestries and chandeliers and lush carpeted floors and giant canopied beds. There was fresh fruit, warm pastries, and bottles of wine on the table, and the air was filled with sweet-scented incense.

We had been there less than a minute when a gaggle of tailors bustled in with fabric, pins, and measuring cords—jerking our arms and legs, measuring our girth and necks and thighs and arms, and the width of our shoulders, all the while chattering about colors, textures, and cuts of cloth, as they jotted down notes and then bustled out again to tailor our clothes for the evening.

After they left, Demetri and I grabbed some pastries and threw ourselves on the giant, soft beds and relaxed, letting the stress of travel and meeting King Helios drain out of us. The pastries were delicious, and we rested only a few minutes before the door burst open again and servants wheeled in two golden tubs full of steaming water.

They pulled us from our beds, stripped off our filthy clothes, and dunked and scrubbed us with brushes and scented oils. I had endured that kind of cleansing a number of times, having grown up in a royal household, but the experience was completely new for Demetri and he was not happy about it. Two of the servants had to be carried out, unconscious, and two others quickly learned that it would be better to let Demetri wash himself.

Then it was thick towels and robes, quick grooming of hair and nails, and then the tailors burst back into our room with completed formal clothes that had been made to fit us perfectly. Demetri was grumbling as we put on our crisp, white shirts with buttons up to the chin, slick black trousers, sharp formal coats, and polished black boots. My coat was a royal purple (which matched my eyes) with long coat tails, while Demetri's was a deep blue (it didn't match his eyes, but who cares). We stood in front of the great, gilded mirror, and I must admit that I looked pretty incredible. (Demetri looked okay).

A servant announced from the hallway that it was time for the ball, so we left our room and knocked on Sierra's door. "Hey Sierra, we've got to go the dance now!" Demetri said, quite impatiently.

Sierra opened the door wearing a stunning red dress with gold lace trimmings. She was sparkling clean—she'd obviously had a bath, too—and her hair had been styled in a way I never would have imagined (don't ask me to describe it). She was wearing jewelry and that incredible dress, and a shy smile.

For some reason I had a hard time breathing for a moment.

Sierra sighed, "I don't like these colors. They're not me. I usually wear darker colors like you two are wearing."
I blinked a couple of times and then chuckled. "Well, they look pretty, uh, fine on you. Anyway, these aren't exactly our clothes, either. I mean, I'll bet Demetri would rather be wearing pink than blue."

Sierra chuckled, showing a hint of her fangs. "Really, Demetri? A pink coat?"

"Ha ha ha!" Demetri laughed sarcastically. "Yeah, right. Me wear a pink coat. Septimus is the one who should be wearing a pink...sweater or something..." He trailed off lamely, then tried to change the subject. "What are we doing standing around here? We're supposed to be at the ball!"

As we walked to the great hall where the party was taking place, I was behind Sierra and noticed how the dress made her arms look slender, her back narrow, and her neck graceful. I had to admit that she looked better than I did, and it was making my head spin. (But on the other hand, she probably couldn't pull off bed head the way I could).

Then we entered the hall and saw an explosion of color. There were people dressed in spectacular finery, dancing and laughing; there were servants milling about with trays of food and drink; and there were musicians with all kinds of string and wood instruments playing orchestral music. Lokir was surrounded by ladies, but when he saw us walk in he broke away from them and made his way over to us through the crowds. He flashed his disarming smile, and I thought I saw Sierra blush a little.

"Welcome, you three! My father hopes you all enjoy yourselves before you leave tomorrow. The food is exquisite, and the more you drink, the better you will dance!" He waved some servants over who were carrying trays of colorful hors d'oeuvres and fluted goblets full of a bubbling golden liquid.

I smiled. "Sounds great, but I'm not one for dancing, I'm afraid."

Still, I grabbed a drink from the platter that a servant offered me, and Demetri also took one while conversing with Lokir.

"Yeah, me too." Demetri said. "I'm more of a blacksmith or a fighter than a dancer."

Lokir chuckled. "That's quite alright. You don't have to dance. But Septimus, I've been meaning to ask you...are you and Sierra courting?"

I froze at Lokir's question, and choked a little on my drink, but they didn't probably didn't notice. "What? No, no, no, I assure you that we're just friends. Anyway, I think you should ask Demetri that question." I said slyly.

Demetri's face turned red again. "No, I'm not courting Sierra!"

Lokir chuckled "Neither of you? Well, that's splendid! Then, Sierra," he said, taking her hand and looking her in the eye, "you look absolutely ravishing! You must dance with me."

Demetri was taking a drink at that moment, and he suddenly coughed, spraying the side of my face. "What!?" Demetri said in alarm.

I was a little annoyed as I took a cloth napkin from a tray and wiped my face.

Lokir smiled. "Oh, see now! He's jealous."

I looked at Demetri, who grabbed the napkin from my hand and wiped his mouth, then dropped it on the floor.

"Uh-oh, Lokir," I chuckled nervously. "I think you've hit a nerve."

Demetri handed his drink to me, and I noticed his jaw was clenched. He took a step closer to Lokir with his ears burning red and a fierce look in his eye. "Oh yeah?"

Demetri then held his hand out stiffly to Sierra. "Sierra, will you dance with me?" He asked, still staring at Lokir.

Lokir's smile turned into a grimace. "You can't do that; I asked first. Besides, I thought you were more of a blacksmith than a dancer."

Demetri's forced smile made him look a little crazed. "You didn't ask her, you commanded her. You can't force her to dance with you."

"I don't know if you realize this, but you're in my kingdom. And besides, I'm not forcing her to dance with me." Lokir scoffed.

Demetri smiled mockingly at Lokir. "I don't know if words mean different things in your kingdom than they do in the rest of the world, but when you tell someone they must do something, you aren't asking, you're telling."

Lokir was now furious. "Enough! We'll let Sierra choose whom to dance with."

Demetri and Lokir both looked at Sierra with their hands stretched out toward her. Sierra was red with embarrassment, obviously something like this had never happened to her before.

Sierra looked from one to the other, then shook her head. "Sorry, Lokir and Demetri, but I think I'm going to dance with...Septimus."

I felt a surge of...what? I don't know, but I dropped both of the drinks I was holding. The shattering of glass startled both Lokir and Demetri, but Sierra seemed to be trying not to laugh. I stepped aside as servants quickly scurried over to clean up the broken glass and spilled liquid.

"Septimus?" Sierra said, reaching out a slender hand toward me.

"What the catfish!? I don't even know how to dance!"

"Come on. This is for world peace." Sierra sighed and took my hand, then literally dragged me to the dance floor where other guests were dancing a waltz that looked terribly complicated. Meanwhile Lokir and Demetri were exchanging insults, but at least they weren't fighting.

Sierra pulled me almost to the middle of the dance floor and we were surrounded by dozens of couples that were mincing and twirling around us.

We stopped and I groaned. "Wait a minute! Don't I get a say in this?"

Sierra chuckled. "Sure. Shall we dance now?"

"I told you, I don't know how to dance!" I was trying to whisper, but it came out louder than I intended and I heard laughter from the people around us.

Sierra smiled. "It easy. Just hold my hand like this, and then put that hand and my waist, right there. Now we'll just move to the music."

I was trying to hide my trembling, and it took all my strength not to turn and flee, but I'm proud to admit that I didn't pass out (like I did on the battlefield). We started dancing and I danced terribly, but I squared my shoulders and bore the shame of my awkwardness until the extremely long song was over.

"Why did you choose me?" I asked, as we bumped into one couple after another. "I didn't even ask you to dance."

"Well, I guess I couldn't take their arguing, so I chose you." She said.

"Why would you choose me over the charming Prince Lokir?" I tried to sound flippant.

Sierra laughed. "Please. Don't you think I have better judgement than that? I know his type."

For some reason that made me feel much better. "Sierra, don't tell Demetri that I told you this...but I'm pretty sure he likes you."

Sierra smiled. "Oh, don't worry. I already knew that."

I chuckled. "You did? Demetri only told me."

"Yeah, well he didn't tell you very quietly, did he? My kind has pretty good hearing." Sierra said.

I looked at the delicate curve of her pointed ears, and then the smooth skin of her cheek and the redness of her lips, and was feeling like my knees might buckle, so I changed the subject. Thankfully I remembered a question I had been meaning to ask her since we got here.

"Sierra, where's this historian we came here for?" I asked. "And who is he, exactly?"

"Oh, his name is Julius Aurelius. He has been a friend to the kingdom of the Moon for years."

"Really? In this city? Where the king hates, uh, your kind?"

"He's a scholar of history and languages, quite open-minded, and very—"

Suddenly the doors to the hall burst open and four city guards marched in carrying a wobbling old man on a stretcher and demanding to see the king. Everyone stopped dancing and talking, and the musicians stopped playing their music. The man on the stretcher wasn't moving—in fact, his eyes were rolled back in his head and his tongue was lolling out of his open mouth.

Demetri approached us and Sierra gasped, just as the king started shouting. "What is the meaning of this? Bursting into my hall and disrupting my party with a filthy corpse!"

"My lord! Please forgive this intrusion, but we have interrogated this traitor, Julius Aurelius." He spat the man's name. "We were bringing him to you so he could make an urgent confession, but unfortunately he died on the way up the stairs. Still, we have his body as proof that we are telling the truth! All four of us are witnesses—"

"Witnesses of what?! Speak quickly, and if I don't like what you say, I will send you to the interrogators, and you will suffer much longer and much more miserably than this old fool did!"

"But, we are the interrogat-" One them started before being shushed by the others, and interrupted by the lead guard.

"My king! The traitor Julius Aurelius spoke of a Vampire girl traveling here to meet him...to discuss some ancient weapon. And he said the girl would be accompanied by none other than...Prince Septimus of the Kingdom of the Sky!"

The king looked shocked for a moment, then looked around and gazed right at us. At that moment every head in the hall turned to stare at us.

"You're certain of this?" The king said in a gravelly voice.

"Father, this is madness!" Lokir interjected. "Don't listen to them."

"Silence, Lokir!"

"But Father, they are just trying to—"

"I said silence!" The king raised a fist as if he were about to strike is son, then slowly lowered it, shaking his head and turned back to the guards. "You all swear that this is true, that Julius Aurelius was a traitor and a spy for the Vampires, and Septimus Legion has brought a Vampire spy right into my court?"

"We stake our lives on the truth of it, Sire." The guard said, bowing his head gravely.

The king's face darkened and twisted into a ball of rage.

"No, Father! Please stop and think about what you are doing." Lokir said quickly. "We want an alliance with the Kingdom of the Sky, not war. What will happen if you—"

The king ignored Lokir and stabbed a finger in our direction, then let out a roar. "A Vampire dares enter my kingdom!? Seize her! And Prince Septimus! And his friend Demetri! They are traitors for bringing a filthy Vampire into my city and into my home!"

Everyone was still gawking at us, and nobody moved.

"Because of this treachery, I decree that from this day forth, the kingdoms of the Sun and the Sky shall be enemies, until all kingdoms are brought to ruin at the end of the world!"

"No, Father!" Lokir pleaded. "This is madness!"

The king reached out with one hand and grabbed his son by the throat, while the other was still pointing at us. He jabbed his finger in our direction half a dozen times while his face started turning purple and looked like it might explode.

"What are you waiting for??" He finally blurted out. "Arrest them and take them to be executed!"

This wasn't a good situation—in fact it was worse than dancing. Our only way out of this was to run, so I signaled Sierra and Demetri in a totally secret way, so the guards wouldn't know my plan, which was to grab both of them and start racing for the door while yelling, "Run!!!"

The party guests were so shocked that they moved out of our way, and we ran right through the great doors with a dozen guards in close pursuit. Of course I had no plan, other than to get away as fast as we could.

Demetri looked infuriated with me. "Are you kidding me, Septimus! Run? You were supposed to yell Babycakes!"

"What!?" I shouted, as we pounded down the corridor. "Babycakes!? Since when!?"

We turned a corner and began racing up a flight of stairs. "Since we were 6 years old!"

We knocked over a suit of armor at the top of the stairs, sending it tumbling down toward our pursuers. We quickly turned a corner and ran down another hallway.

"How am I supposed to remember that?!" I shouted.

We turned another corner, and I realized that I was lost. This castle was such a maze! There had to be a flight of stairs back down to the first level that would lead to an exit. We ran down one hallway, and then another. There were no stairs leading down that I could find, and Demetri wasn't quite as fast as Sierra and I, and he was falling behind.

Demetri was slowing as he shouted, "You should remember be-"

Just then a guard tackled Demetri, which left me running with Sierra, and a whole troop of guards still running behind us.

"Septimus! We lost Demetri!" Sierra yelled to me, even though she was running right beside me.

This was a disaster. I had no plan, and now we were going to have to find a way to escape, then come back and rescue Demetri...but I didn't want Sierra to panic.

"It's okay, we can't afford to stop!" I said. "Now come this way!"

We turned another corner and down a wider hallway that I thought must lead to a stairwell. I grabbed Sierra's hand and was tugging her to get her to run faster.

"But Septimus, he's your best friend you can't just lea-"

Yes...it got worse. Guards came from a side hallway and they got Sierra too. Her hand was pulled away from mine and I barely dodged their reach. So now I was just running by myself.

There was no stairwell at the end of the hallway, but I turned the corner and pulled a great door open just enough to squeeze through, and found myself in a large hall. I started racing toward the far door—surely there was a stairway there—when it burst open and guards came rushing in. I looked behind me and they were pouring in from that side also.

That's when my Elven agility really kicked in. Before I knew it, I was jumping over tables, climbing onto a platform, and then leaping for a balcony, which I just barely caught onto. I pulled myself up, climbed over the railing, and ran through an archway, with half a battalion clambering up after me.

This was madness. I had no idea where I was going and no real chance of escape, but I was so full of adrenalin that I wasn't about to stop and let myself get caught.

I ran through two more hallways, but could not shake my pursuers, so I resorted to one of my best talents – sass. I started hopelessly yelling back to the guards. "Okay! I will kindly accept your surrender, if you hand my friends over unharmed!"

A cheeky guard yelled back to me, "Not a chance Septimus! You're a traitor! You will be beheaded for this!"

"I will be headed for the exit if you will show me the way!" I shouted.

"Your head will be rolling in the street by this time tomorrow!" The guard retorted.

At this point I was cursing myself for running up the stairs of the castle and not out of the castle, which was seeming more and more like a foolish mistake. I was already on the third floor, racing through the hallways, looking desperately for an escape...until I came to a great window and saw that this wing was overlooking the Inland Sea. So logically, I ran to the window, threw open the latch, and hurled myself out into churning sea below.

Chapter Eight: An Old Friend

I woke from blackness into what appeared to be a dimly lit, tavern guest room. I had no idea where I was or how I arrived here. I had a vague memory of being immersed in cold, black water, and then...nothing. What had happened?

I was on my back, and I tried to roll off the straw mattress onto my feet, but my legs must have been asleep because I couldn't feel them, and they couldn't support my weight. I crashed to the floor and fell on my right arm, which sent an electrifying jolt of pain through my body. I yelled out involuntarily, and rolled over onto my back on the floor, holding my aching arm. My cry alerted someone, because the door swung open and a cloaked figure rushed to my side and began helping me sit up.

"Are you alright?" I couldn't see the cloaked person's face, but from the pitch of their voice I knew it was a woman. However, the sound was muffled—probably still had water in my ears.

"You're finally awake." She said.

I was awake, obviously. "I'm alright." I grumbled.

"Why does my arm hurt so bad? Where am I?"

"You're here, and you're safe." The cloaked woman chuckled. "And, if you would have stopped to make sure that you were okay, you would have noticed that your arm is injured."

I looked down at my right forearm and noticed that it was wrapped in a bloodstained cloth. Injury? I had cut my arm on something...how had that happened? Vague memories started to seep into my mind...running, yelling, getting separated from my friends, jumping out of a window...wait, my friends! My friends were in trouble! They had been captured by the insane king's guards, and they were going to be executed!

Suddenly I didn't care about the cut on my arm...oh yeah, I cut it on the steel window frame when I leapt from the castle into the sea...no, that didn't matter! How long had I been unconscious? Was I too late to save them already? I needed to get to my friends!

I grabbed onto the woman's cloak. "Listen! I need to know where I am and how to get back to the castle! My friends need me!"

"Shhhhh," the cloaked woman gently took my hand and pulled it away from her cloak. "Everything is going to be alright. I found you unconscious on the beach last night, so I brought you to this tavern. I couldn't believe it was you! I carried you myself, dragged you a little. Anyway, I knew the tavern keeper was a kind man, and he dressed you in dry clothes and bandaged your wound while I attended to other matters."

Why hadn't the tavern keeper healed me? Wasn't he a mage? I was confused, obviously. "What are you talking about? Who are you?"

"You don't recognize me?" She asked, and finally removed her hood.

I recognized her immediately! She had long blonde hair, silver eyes, and pointed ears. Yes, she was of the race of Elves, like me. In fact, her name was Olivia Legion—and she was my cousin!

She used to hang out with me and Demetri when we were younger, but as she grew older our interests diverged. She was now an accomplished archer who had been traveling the kingdoms competing in archery tournaments for a couple of years. She looked exactly the same as I remembered, but a little older. She was wearing all dark colors—blacks and greys—and she was obviously wearing a black hooded cloak.

The shock of seeing her after all these years made me forget what was going on. "Olivia!? What are you doing here?"

Olivia smiled. "Saving you, obviously. Mind you, we are inside the city walls in the Kingdom of the Sun, so you might want to keep your voice down so we aren't overheard. The guards are still looking for you."

"What!? You're kidding me! I've got to go," I said, struggling to my feet, and testing my legs to make sure they weren't going to fail me again.

"It was really nice seeing you, but I need to get going, before my friends are executed."

I started hobbling toward the door, but Olivia jumped up and blocked the exit. "Septimus! You silly fool, you haven't changed at all! Will you stop and think for just a moment?"

"I'll think on the way." I growled.

"On the way to where? Where do you think you're going? You don't even know what part of the city you're in. You don't know where your friends are being held..."

I hated it when she made sense like that.

"You don't have a plan. You don't have any weapons. You don't have a disguise. Your arm is still injured—"

"Yeah, and why is that?" I snapped. "Every tavern keeper knows enough magery to heal flesh wounds. I thought you said he was a good person?"

Olivia rolled her eyes. "He is a good person, which is why he needs your permission to do magery on you."

"Afraid of getting blamed if he made a mistake, eh? Where is this tavern keeper?" I asked impatiently.

"You stay right here, I'll get him." Olivia said.

She left for a moment and I was tempted to leave, but she was right that I didn't know where I was or where I was going. I was definitely going to need a lot of help if I was going to rescue my friends.

She returned shortly with the tavern keeper. He was an older fellow, his hair and his long beard were as white as bone. He was wearing a long wool coat, which was mostly covered in patches. But what stood out most prominently were his enormous, pointed ears—he was of the race of Elves, like Olivia and me.

"Septimus, this is my friend, Philo." Olivia said. Philo had a kindly look in his eye and a broad smile on his face. "Oh, so good to see that you're alright, my lord." He slightly bowed as he said it.

I nervously chuckled. "You know who I am? Well, I am in your debt for taking me in and keeping me safe last night. Would you be willing to do me another favor and heal my arm?"

Philo smiled even wider. "Oh, it would be an honor! Let's remove that bandage and I'll get to work."

The bandage was difficult to remove because it stuck to some of the dried blood, but once it was pulled free I felt the burning rush of air, and new pain surged through my arm. I looked down at it and felt a little dizzy. I was missing a chunk of flesh on my forearm, and I could practically see bone.

Philo furrowed his brow and grunted to himself, but he didn't seem alarmed. He gently raised my arm—which was painful because any movement at all hurt like crazy—and then examined my arm all around.

"I know what to do," he said finally. "Olivia, close the door and then I'll need you to hold his arm still. Lord Prince, you will need something to bite on—we don't want you to bite your tongue."

"Why would I bite my tongue?" I asked, not sure I wanted to know the answer.

"The pain will be severe," he said. "You are going to scream and you are going to grit your teeth. I don't want your tongue to get in the way."

My arm was already throbbing—I wasn't sure I wanted pain any more severe than this. He produced a thick leather strap that I put between my teeth and bit down on. Olivia knelt beside me and carefully gripped my forearm on both sides of the wound. Her hands were stronger than I remembered. Philo produced a dark phial of black potion that gave off a strong odor of iron.

"On the count of three," Philo said. "One...two…"

I didn't hear him say "three." The moment he poured the black potion on my wound, I felt excruciating pain at the same moment I heard a deafening noise. It took me a moment to realize it was my screaming.

"Gaaaaahhhhhhhhggggg!" I yelled through gritted teeth, biting down savagely on the leather strap.

Olivia held my arm tightly and I tried not to convulse as the horrible burning continued for about a minute. The wound bubbled black tar, and Philo was whispering words I couldn't hear, and eventually the burning started to subside. It lessened and then quickly turned into coldness, like ice was forming in my bloodstream.

Philo placed his hand over the wound and continued his whispered chant, over and over, and then he raised his hand and the black tar was gone. I could see pink sinews of flesh forming and growing like webs across the gap, until the hole was filled and new layers of skin spread across the top. It now looked as good as new, but Philo kept chanting for another minute before he finally stopped and then checked my arm.

"There you have it. A full recovery, my lord!" He said. Olivia released my arm and smiled at me, and I removed the leather strap from my mouth.

"Thank you, kind sir." I felt my arm and the pain was now completely gone. There wasn't even a scar where the wound had been. "I've never seen a potion like that. What was that black liquid?"

"Truth be told, it wasn't a potion, my lord. It was Vampire blood." Philo said.

"Wait, what? Am I going to turn into a vampire now!?" I said in alarm.

"No, no, no, calm yourself. You can only become a Vampire from their bites. Anyone who has studied Vampires knows that their blood has healing properties—it is how they heal themselves when they are injured." Philo said.

"Interesting, I always wondered—"

Suddenly I was interrupted by Olivia. "Septimus, your arm is healed, now it's time to get going! Don't you need to save your friends?"

"Yes, but as you pointed out before, I don't know where they are or anything that has happened to them—"

"Of course you don't, Silly, but I do! What do you think I was doing last night while you were sleeping?"

I thanked Philo again and he wished us well as we put on our cloaks and left the tavern, heading back to the castle as Olivia explained what she had in mind.

Chapter Nine: A Change of Plans

Olivia and I were almost at the castle. We were walking with our hoods up and faces down, trying to blend in with a group of people who were ascending the many-gated ramp up to the castle. We were two Elves who would have otherwise stood out in the capital city of Men, and so far we hadn't had any trouble passing the clusters of guards along the way.

However, we noticed that there was a larger contingent of guards at the gate at the top of the ramp that were checking people one by one, requiring them to remove their hats or lower their hoods. They must have been looking for someone...probably me! We slowed our pace and let the group of people we were following move far ahead of us, then we stopped to adjust our plans.

"I wasn't expecting this." Olivia said. "If we try to get in, they'll find out who you are!"

She had learned last night that Demetri and Sierra were being held in the castle dungeon instead of the prison by the docks, or the jail in the outer court. That made sense because Demetri and Sierra weren't pirates or petty thieves; they were being charged with treason against the king, so they were being held in his dungeon. But that also meant that we were going to have to get into the castle in order to get them out. Olivia had done it last night, but now that I was with her it was more complicated.

We needed a plan. We needed allies to help us. Allies... I suddenly had an idea. "Prince Lokir!"

"The king's son? What about him?" Olivia was puzzled.

"He can help us! He doesn't like Demetri much, but he didn't want us to be arrested last night. He tried to stop the king from ordering us to be captured and executed."

"That's nice, but you can't get to him. You would have to go into the castle." Olivia said reasonably.

"That's right. I can't get to him, but you can. Olivia, how do you feel about going into the castle to convince Prince Lokir to sneak us in?"

"What makes you think he will listen to me?"

"I know he'll listen to you because I know his weakness—beautiful women. You should have seen him drooling over Sierra last night. You walk in there and turn on your feminine Elvish charm, and you'll have him eating out of the palm of your hand." I said.

"Gross!" Olivia pretended to gag. "I don't want him eating out of my hand or drooling on it."

"I'm positive this will work. Do you have a better plan?"

Olivia stomped her foot in frustration. "No. Okay, fine. Where should I look for him?"

"I have no idea." I admitted. "Yesterday we were in the throne room, the guest wing, the banquet hall, and a bunch of other places that I barely remember because that place is a freaking maze."

"Then how am I ever going to find him?"

"Easy." I chuckled. "He only likes two things: fighting Orcs and cavorting with women. There aren't any Orc around so if you go where the women are, he will find you."

"Well, where—" Olivia began, then shrugged and said, "Never mind."

I watched Olivia walk to the gate at the top of the ramp and remove her hood. She conversed with the guards briefly and they let her pass. When she disappeared from sight I casually blended in at the back of a group of people walking back down the ramp, past the other guarded gates where the security was more lax. I didn't want to be standing around on the ramp for too long and attract attention.

I waited in an alley next to a pub near the base of the ramp for more than an hour before I saw Olivia coming back down—walking with Prince Lokir!

I signaled Olivia and then went deeper into the alley and waited for them to join me.

"Hello Septimus! So you want me to sneak you into the castle?" Lokir asked, beaming (and talking way too loudly).

"Hello, Lokir. Yes, we need your help getting into the castle to save my friends. But we're not going to get much sneaking done if you shout our plan to everyone."

Lokir laughed. "That isn't going to be a problem."

"What do you mean?" I asked. "Are you going to betray us?"

"Of course not!" Lokir's expression morphed from a toothy grin into a sad puppy look. "How could you think such a thing?"

"We've been talking it through, and he's right." Olivia sighed, which caused Prince Lokir to grin again. "There are all kinds of ways to disguise us and sneak us into the castle, but not into the dungeons."

"Security there is much too tight." Lokir said. "You're going to have to trust me on this, but if you want to get to your friends, you're going to have to let yourself get caught."

He might as well have told me that the plan was to turn ourselves into butterflies and flutter our way in to the dungeon. I realized my mouth was gaping open, but before closing it I said, "That's the stupidest thing I've ever heard!"

"Septimus, wait." Olivia said.

But I wasn't listening to her. "Really? That's your plan? To get us thrown in prison so we can all be executed together??"

Olivia put her hand on my shoulder. "Septimus, if this works out right, we're going to get your friends out, and we'll be able to escape the city."

"But in order to do that, you're going to have to trust me." Lokir said. "And there will be a price."

So that was it. There was always a catch. "A price?" I asked.

"Well, nothing of worth is ever free. Don't you agree?"

Now we were getting to the truth. He knew I was a prince, too, and that my father had great wealth. "So what do you want?" I asked. "A ransom paid by my father? A title and a deed of land in the Kingdom of the Sky?"

"No, nothing like that." Lokir smiled, then turned and looked earnestly at Olivia. "I realized after I met you today that I couldn't live another moment without you. You must become my wife!"

"What!?" Olivia said, stumbling back against the wall of the pub. "No, no, no, I'm not marrying you!"

"Lokir, don't you think you're rushing into things?" I said, trying to be helpful.

Lokir didn't seem to have heard anything we said. He was still gazing at Olivia with moon eyes. "It was never clear to me before today..."

"You never met her before today." I said.

"...but now that I see you Olivia, I realize that I must have you for my wife!"

"Lokir!" I said, snapping my fingers in front of his face. "Come on, wake up! Your father would never let you marry a girl who you threw into prison."

He blinked a couple of times and looked at me, and then he shrugged. "Fine! I will settle for a kiss."

That seemed reasonable. Lokir and I both looked at Olivia for confirmation.

"Seriously?" Olivia sighed. "Fine, but not until after we free our friends!"

"Of course!" Lokir said. "But how about a quick one now for good luck, and then the real one after they're free?"

"After! The deal is that you free them first!" Olivia said, but then laughed. "You are unbelievable!"

"Why, thank you. Women often have a difficult time believing that someone as amazing as me could actually be real. So we have a deal, then?" Lokir asked.

Olivia nodded.

"Yes we have a deal, now let's go!" I said.

"Of course." Lokir said. "After you."

We walked out of the alley and Lokir immediately began shouting, "Guards! I found Septimus Legion and his accomplice!"

Lokir was standing behind me, holding my arms behind my back, and holding Olivia by the hood of her cloak. We pretended to struggle while the guards came running towards us, then gave up when they laid powerful hands on us.

"Take them to the dungeons!" Lokir said pushing us roughly.

"Certainly, my lord." One of the guards said.

Then something happened that we didn't plan. The guard hit me in the head with the hilt of his sword, and everything went black.

Chapter Ten: The Escape

I woke up with a headache and on a damp, stone bed in a jail cell with Demetri and Olivia. Demetri was trying to find a way to open the cell door, while Olivia was sitting on the floor, leaning against the wall of the cell and dozing.

I was extremely relieved that Demetri was alive, but Sierra was nowhere to be seen. I sat up on the bed, my head pounding.

"Where's Sierra?" I mumbled.

"She's here." Demetri said, then turned around and stared at me wide-eyed. "Hey, you're alive!"

"Yeah, so are you!" I noticed he had a large bruise around one eye. "And you're looking prettier than usual." I put my hand on the back of my head and felt like I was going to black out again.

"Well, I wish I could say the same for you." Demetri said. "Some friend you are! You know, after you abandoned me last night I was hoping they had treated you the same way they did the Orcs down by the river."

Demetri scowled at me for a moment, and then broke into a grin. He came over and grabbed me in a hug and slapped me on the back. "You're an idiot for getting yourself captured. You should have just gone home."

"It's good to see you, too." I said, my head pounding more than ever.

Just then Olivia woke up. "Septimus, you're alive!" She stood up and hugged me, too.

"Why do you guys keep saying that?" I asked. "Did I look dead?"

"Well the guard did hit you in the head pretty hard. We didn't know if you were going to wake up from that." Olivia said, then turned to Demetri. "And you weren't even worried about your best friend!"

"Bah, I knew he was going to be okay." Demetri said. "He makes the best plans, and they always work out."

For some reason both Demetri and Olivia started laughing, but I didn't think there was anything funny about it.

"My plans usually do work out." I said.

"Septimus, we know you. You don't actually make plans." Olivia said. "You come up with harebrained ideas, and then you rush out and do something completely different."

"How is that not a plan?" I asked, genuinely perplexed. Olivia rolled her eyes.

"So...I guess we're all pretty much dead now." Demetri said. "I'm glad to see you, but it's too bad you two had to get yourselves caught."

"Demetri, hold on. There's nothing to worry about—we have a plan." I said.

Demetri groaned. "No offense, Septimus, but I hope it was Olivia's plan. I've seen how yours work out."

"Ha ha ha. So, you said Sierra is here? I don't see her..." I said, still rubbing my head.

"Oh, the guards gave her her own cell." Demetri said.

"What? Why does she have her own cell?" I asked.

"I don't know, ask the guards." Demetri said.

That wasn't a bad idea. "Alright." I said, and walked to the cell bars and looked around the dungeon. The dungeon was a very long corridor filled with dozens of cells, there were two levels of cells, one above the other.

Just then the dungeon door opened and two guards walked in and sat down at a table right next to the door. Without even looking in our direction they began playing cards.

"Hey! Guards!" I shouted.

One of the guards slapped his cards down on the table and slowly looked in our direction. "What is it, Prince Septimus?" He asked in a mocking tone. "Are you uncomfortable? You want me to fluff your pillow?"

The other guard thought that was pretty funny and barked out an obnoxious laugh.

"You know it wouldn't kill you guys to toss us a few pillows!" Demetri shouted. "We're going to be executed soon anyway, so what's the harm?"

"Shut up or you'll be wishing your execution had already happened!" The other guard said.

"Forget the pillows," I said. "I just have one question for you."

"Just the one? Let me guess: you're going to ask if I will open the door and let you go?" The first guard said mockingly again.

"No, that would be silly. I just want to know why Sierra Evans has her own cell." I said.

He chuckled. "Well isn't it obvious? She's a Vampire! She's dangerous and needs to be held in our most secure cell. Now quit your yapping! I've got a card game to win." Then he turned around and picked up his cards again, muttering under his breath.

I turned to look at Olivia and Demetri. "They think she's dangerous? I guess they don't know that she can't use her Vampire powers." I said.

"You can't blame them for being cautious." Olivia said.

All of a sudden we heard a loud boom from the hallway. We were all startled, and the sound echoed through the whole dungeon. We looked through the bars and saw that the dungeon door had flown open and had hit the stone wall.

Then we saw Lokir appear in the doorway down the cellblock, holding a silver platter with three silver goblets and a large bottle of wine. Both of the guards had already leaped out of their seats and had drawn their swords to defend against an attack, but when they saw it was Prince Lokir, they lowered their swords and bowed to him.

"My apologies! I hope I didn't startle you." Lokir grinned. "My hands were full and I had to push the door open with my foot. I guess I don't know my own strength." He laughed, and the guards forced a cautious laugh as well.

"My prince, we weren't expecting you." One of the guards said as they both sheathed their swords.

"Of course you weren't. I rarely come down to this miserable place—it's so depressing—but after I caught Septimus and his cousin today I started thinking about the guards who have to work down here. It must be awful for you to have to be with criminals all day…"

"Not at all, my lord—I mean—we do work hard, but we know this is important work and we're proud to do it."

"That's right, we do our duty. Nothing to complain about here!" The other guard added hastily.

"You do your jobs so well that nobody has ever escaped from the king's dungeon! Not in all these years has a single prisoner so much as tried to escape. You should be proud of that accomplishment!"

"You're too kind, lord. We ain't the only guards down here. There's others who do their duty just as well as us." The guard was blushing.

"Yes, well, you make an excellent point. They should all be proud. As a matter of fact, they all deserve some recognition—and I've already expressed my appreciation to several of them. Now it's your turn. I brought you two a little token of my appreciation." Lokir said, smiling broadly as he placed the tray on the table.

"No, no, my prince, that's quite alright. You don't need to give us nothing."

"And we're not allowed to—"

"Oh, I disagree!" Lokir interrupted. "I would like to toast your accomplishments with one of the finest bottles from my father's wine cellar."

"But the captain said—"

"Come now, you've earned this! So I must insist." Lokir said popping open the old bottle and pouring the wine into each of the three goblets. After Lokir was done pouring, a guard reached for one of the goblets, but Lokir swatted his hand and grabbed it first.

"This one is my personal goblet." Lokir said.

"They all look the same." One of the guards mumbled, but Lokir ignored him. When all three were holding their brimming goblets, trying to hold them carefully so they didn't slosh, Lokir began his toast.

"Most noble guards of the deepest dungeon of the Kingdom of the Sun," he nodded to each of them, "I salute and honor you for your valiant service in guarding the worst villains of the land before they receive the justice of horrible deaths!

Both of the guards were smiling bashfully now.

"I salute and honor your bravery, your diligence, and your sharp senses that you employ so valiantly in the service of your king!"

They nodded happily.

"I salute and honor you for your loyal service here in the dark and miserable depths where you labor day after day—without complaint—in a stinking hole that smells like a cesspit!"

They looked at him blankly for a moment, then shrugged their shoulders and nodded.

"Cheers!" Lokir said raising his goblet into the air.

"Cheers!" Both the guards said, also raising their goblets into the air.

Then they all drank deeply from their goblets.

"This really is good wine." Lokir said, draining his goblet and then placing it back on the tray.

He reached out to slap one of the guards on the shoulder, but he barely touched him when both guards suddenly collapsed. They crumpled right onto the table, which promptly tipped over. They hit the hard floor with a loud smack and didn't move at all. Lokir quickly bent over them and took the keys from one of the belts, then walked with a swagger to our cell door.

"Alright, time to go my friends!" Lokir said while unlocking the door. "But first things first. I'll be collecting that kiss now, Olivia."

"We're still in the dungeon." She said. "You'll get your kiss when we're free."

"Wait, what?" Demetri said.

"Later, Demetri." I said. "Lokir, lead us to Sierra's cell."

He seemed a little grumpy about not getting his kiss yet, but he led us down the corridor past the guards sprawled on the floor next to the overturned table.

"What did you do to them?" I asked. "You didn't kill them?"

"No, of course not. I lined the inside of their goblets with a sleeping potion. I've heard that it tastes quite sweet, but I've never tried it myself."

"How long does it last?"

"Not long. Maybe ten minutes?"

"Then why aren't we running?"

We rushed down the corridor to the very end which had a large steel door with a small grate at the top. Lokir unlocked the door and slowly opened it, for it was very heavy. We gazed in and saw Sierra standing with her back against the far wall. When she saw that it was us, she rushed forward and gave me a hug.

"I can't believe it!" She said. "You're alive!"

"Yeah, I know it's a miracle that we're all alive." I said as she released me.

"But we're not going to be alive for long if we don't get out of here!" Demetri said. "That crazy king is still planning to execute us."

Lokir was pouting. "Hey, I'm the one doing the rescuing here. No hug for me?"

"Sure, why not." Demetri said, grabbing his hand and pulling him in for a bro hug. "Okay, now get us out of here!"

Thankfully Lokir must have realized that there wasn't time for complaining, so he led us out of the cell block, past a couple of other unconscious guards who looked like they might be starting to stir, and up a flight of stairs. He used the keys to lock each barred door we passed through, as well as the barred gate at the top of the stairs. That would hopefully delay any pursuit after the guards woke up.

Lokir led us to the jailor's storeroom, which was full of baskets of clothes and crates of confiscated items that I assumed had been the property of prisoners. I quickly found my sword, cloak, and satchel in a basket.

"I'm missing my bag." Sierra said worriedly.

"Don't worry, we'll find it." I said while looking through baskets and crates.

Then all of a sudden I thought I heard a woman's voice coming from one of the crates. I must have been losing my mind, but I went over to the crate and lifted the lid, and a blinding green light burst out of it. I shielded my eyes, and when I looked again, I saw Sierra's bag. Sitting next to the bag was a green orb, about the size of a peach, which was glowing brightly.

"Hey Sierra, I found your bag." I said. "Do you want to tell us about this?"

Sierra ran over to me. "Don't touch that!" Sierra said while stuffing the orb into her bag.

"What was that?" I asked

"Nothing…don't worry about it." Sierra said.

Yeah, sure, I thought. There's nothing that makes you worry more about something than saying "don't worry about it." That green orb was glowing, which meant it was a magical object. Sierra was carrying around a magical object that she hadn't told us about, and clearly didn't want us to know about. I wanted more answers, but she wasn't offering information, and unfortunately, now wasn't the time to try to pry it out of her.

"Does everyone have what they need?" Lokir asked, and we all nodded. "Okay let's get out of here."

He led us on a winding path through corridors, hidden doors, unused passages, and up and down several staircases, until we finally emerged through a small cellar door, behind the kitchens, that led to a garden path and a hidden door in the garden wall.

Lokir quickly opened the puzzle lock on the door and then swung it open for us. "This leads to an alley that is only three blocks from the West Gate to the city. Put your hoods up and you should be able to walk out without a problem."

"We can't thank you enough for your help, Lokir." I said, gripping his hand.

"That's true. I am the only person who could have gotten you out. Which reminds me...Olivia!"

Olivia forced a smile and took a deep breath. "A deal is a deal." She said.

The kiss was uncomfortable for all of the rest of us, but after it finally ended I thought I saw a hint of a smile on Olivia's face as she looked at Lokir, then shyly looked away.

"Let's head for the gate." I said.

But Sierra shook her head. "Not yet! We can't leave until we have the information that we came here for."

"How are we going to get it now? Your friend, Julius Aurelius, is dead." I said.

"He kept a journal with all his notes. It's got to be hidden someplace in his house. He has a study with a large collection of books. It's probably there." Sierra said desperately.

"Sierra, people are going to be looking for us. Do you even know where he lives?" Demetri asked.

"Don't worry, I know where his house is!" Lokir said. "And for the right price I would be willing to—"

"Take us there!" Sierra said. "We've got to find it quickly."

"You know the price." Lokir said, grinning at Sierra.

"Wait, what?" Olivia said.

"Fine. Let's go!" Sierra said.

"It's not far." Lokir said.

Julius Aurelius's house was in shambles. We should have realized that it would have been ransacked, since he had been accused of spying for the Vampires. The front door was open and hanging at an odd angle, and the inside was a mess. Tables and chairs had been knocked over, the bed was torn apart and the straw mattress had been cut open, and there were clothes, papers, and books all over the floor.

"So what does this journal look like?" I asked. "Have you ever seen it?"

"It's a small book with a black leather cover and a silver clasp. He took it with him everywhere." Sierra said.

"And you don't think the guards confiscated it?" Olivia asked.

"Oh, that reminds me. That sounds just like this journal." Lokir said, pulling a small tattered journal out of his pocket. It had a black cover and a silver clasp.

"Where did you get that?" Sierra asked.

"From the interrogators. They thought it might contain evidence of other conspirators against our kingdom, so I told them I would investigate it myself." Lokir said. "Now Sierra, it's time for you to keep your promise and give me a kiss..."

"I didn't promise to give you a kiss." Sierra said. "I told you to take us here, and you asked if I knew the price. The price is that I don't use my Vampire magic and kill you right here."

I smiled, realizing that she was bluffing, but the look on her face was pretty fierce and convincing.

"I see." Lokir said, his smile fading a little. "In that case, we are even, since you are here in Julius Aurelius's house, and I have not been murdered by Vampire magic."

"That's right." Sierra glared at him. "Now, may I have the journal, please?"

"Ah, you want something else of value that only I can provide." Lokir said, his grin widening again. "You know there is always a price."

"I'm not kissing him again." Olivia mumbled.

"That remains to be seen," Lokir said with a wink, "but that is not what I'm demanding this time. My price is…"

"Here it comes." I said.

"...you must allow me to join you on your adventure!" Lokir said.

We were all stunned for a moment, then Demetri spoke. "You've lost your mind!"

Lokir glared at Demetri. "I am not my father."

I saw that I needed to speak up. "What Demetri is trying to say is that our adventure is going to be extremely dangerous. We could all be killed, even if your father never catches us. And you don't even know what we're doing or where we're going."

Lokir nodded thoughtfully, and then said, "Do any of you know where you're going?"

We all shrugged and looked at Sierra who turned a shade of pink and then shook her head.

"That's what I thought." Lokir grinned again. "None of you know where you're going, so that makes us the same. And as far as the danger is concerned, I've killed dozens of Orcs and fought in several battles. I think that makes me the most qualified person to go on a dangerous adventure."

"Maybe, but do you think your father would approve of this?" Olivia asked.

Lokir laughed. "He'll never find out, and what he doesn't know won't hurt him! Come on, you guys are a lot of fun, and I know you'll appreciate having someone like me around."

We all looked around at each other. Demetri was frowning and Olivia was rolling her eyes, but I could tell Sierra was willing to do just about anything to get that journal.

"Well, it wouldn't hurt to have another sword on our side." I said. "We don't know how long we'll be gone—it could be weeks."

"Or months." Olivia said.

"Or years!" Demetri said.

But Lokir wasn't dissuaded. "It's a deal then!" Lokir said, patting Sierra's hand as he handed her the journal. "Now how about a nice group hug to seal our fellowship? Septimus and Demetri, you can sit this one out if you like."

Everyone ignored him while Sierra opened the journal and flipped through some pages. It took only a minute or two before she said, "Aha! I found it! The hiding place of the ancient sword, *Drocnod*, is in the lost Kingdom of the Stars." Sierra said with excitement.

"What's the Kingdom the the Stars?" Demetri asked.

"And why is it lost?"

"Oh, I've heard of it," Lokir chuckled. "It's a part of an old myth about a lost race of astronomers who studied the stars and created powerful weapons. But they disappeared centuries ago."

"But you think it's just a myth?" I asked.

"Actually, there are artifacts in my father's vaults that I believe must have come from the Kingdom of the Stars – carvings with strange writing, ornate jewelry, a warhammer – but they are extremely rare and have been found scattered in regions as diverse as the Ice Wastes in the North and the Burning Desert in the South."

"It's not a myth." Sierra said. "I know that for a fact."

"So where was this kingdom?" Demetri asked.

"Well that's the problem, isn't it?" Lokir said. "Nobody knows where this kingdom actually was, and there is no way to find it."

Sierra chuckled. "Unless you're a scholar who has learned to decipher their language, and have read the inscriptions on the artifacts people have collected." Sierra said. "It's not lost anymore! The journal says that the Lost Kingdom is in the Silver Mountains. Julius Aurelius has even drawn a map for us!"

Chapter Eleven: The Silver Mountains

We had two more errands before leaving the capital city of the Kingdom of the Sun. First, we had to return to the tavern to get Olivia's things (most importantly her bow), and second, we had to get our horses from the stables. It turned out that Olivia's friend Philo was a great help with both errands.

After Olivia collected her possessions, Philo was very generous in providing us with food and full canteens for our journey, including some blood for Sierra. Afterward he sent two servants with Demetri (who we thought would be the least likely to be recognized by passing guards) to fetch horses for us from the stables.

Once we had loaded our horses we said goodbye to Philo and left the city in two groups—Lokir, Sierra, and Demetri rode out through the South Gate, while Olivia and I rode out through the West gate. This was Olivia's plan, and I must admit it worked pretty well. Nobody suspected us, we got out safely, and we met at the great bridge outside of the city to begin our journey South.

After crossing the great stone bridge that spanned the river, we rode due south for the rest of the day through fields and grasslands that eventually gave way to a dry waste with little vegetation. We camped in a dry creek bed once the sun went down, and ate provisions from our packs. That night we slept wrapped up in our cloaks, because we had lost our tents in the battle with the Orcs. It was a surprisingly cold night, and in the morning we found we had all huddled close together to conserve body heat.

We continued our journey, and by the middle of the second day we could see the mountains in the distance. However, our excitement about seeing the mountains quickly evaporated when we realized how far away they were. We didn't reach them by the end of that day or the next.

By the end of the fourth day we had depleted all of our food and most of our water, and it didn't seem like we were much closer to the mountains.

It was very hot during the day and cold at night, and we were starting to worry about what would happen to us if we ran out of water before we made it to the mountains. We endured another miserable day and a half of travel through the desert, and by that time we were all irritable and short-tempered. Nobody wanted to talk because all that would result were complaints or arguments.

We were tired, starved, and trying to suck the last drop out of our canteens when the landscape finally began to change. Little by little there was more vegetation as we continued south, and we saw birds in the distance. Our horses started picking up the pace, and I suspected they smelled water.

We celebrated when we finally came to a small stream. Our horses walked right into the stream and drank thirstily. We dismounted, laughing and splashing each other in the water, and then drank our fill upstream from where the horses were. We made camp and let the horses rest and graze the rest of that day, and most of the next. Olivia shot several birds and didn't seem capable of missing a target with her bow. She collected, cleaned, and repaired her arrows so they could be used again. We were happy that there was plenty of fresh meat, and we cooked it over a fire as soon as she brought the birds down.

We packed up camp and continued our journey when our horses were sufficiently rested, and we travelled almost another entire day over the foothills that rose up to the base of a great chain of mountains. In the late afternoon Sierra pointed to a canyon and said she thought that we would find a cliff face there with a door that would lead us into the mountain.

I wasn't sure she was reading the map right, but sure enough, we found a cliff face and followed it for half a mile. We came to an enormous facade of pillared buildings carved into the stone, with an open doorway large enough for two wagons to pass through at the same time.

We dismounted and led our horses through the doorway, and once we passed the edge of the light, it was pitch black in the cavernous room. There was a sour smell in the air, and after Demetri had made a small fire to provide a little light and make some torches, it was easy to see where it was coming from. There were shallow channels carved in ornate designs in the stone floor that stretched throughout the cavern, and they were filled with an oily liquid. Demetri had an idea and took a burning brand from the fire and touched it to the oily liquid. Instantly flame filled the channel and raced down the cavern, filling the enormous chamber with an orange glow.

With the whole cavern lit up, we realized it was much larger than we had suspected. In fact it was impossibly large, unless there was some kind of magic supporting the domed ceiling that seemed as high and broad as the sky. Now we could see that there were hundreds of houses carved into the stone in every direction. There were also ramps and staircases, roads and bridges above and below us. This was not just a town, it was a kingdom.

"This place is incredible!" Demetri said.

I nodded. The engineering and crafting magic they must have used to build it were impressive, but it also felt dangerous, like the whole thing could come crashing down at any moment.

"Who would live like this? In the darkness under a mountain." Olivia asked.

"Obviously the people who built it." Lokir said.

"Yeah, but they're not alive now." I pointed out.

"Who were they?" Olivia asked.

"Nobody knows for sure what they called themselves." Sierra said. "Julius Aurelius' notes refer to the Gophrings, the Jarnings, and the Stoneheavers. He wasn't certain if those were clan names or names that referred to the race of people. Most scholars just call them Dwarves, because they were shorter and stockier than Elves or Men. They were skilled miners and craftsmen in these mountains, but now they are extinct because of what they made."

"What did they make?" I asked.

"You mean besides all of this?" Sierra gestured around at the cavern. "You'll see."

She consulted a map in the journal as we walked down the main walkway to the opposite wall from the main entrance. On the opposite wall there were thousands of stairs leading up to a doorway. Perhaps it was because the stairs were so expertly made, or perhaps it was some kind of preserving magic, but the stairs weren't crumbling with age and only had a hint of dust on them. They looked practically new.

By the time we reached the top I was no longer impressed with the workmanship. Wheezing and struggling to catch my breath I was angry that anyone would build such a long staircase. We all had to pause and rest for a while, studying the great stone door at the top, which was covered in ornately carved decorations and runes. I suspected it would be sealed with a magical lock and doubted that we would ever see what was behind it. To my surprise, Sierra walked up to it and pulled the handle, and the heavy door swung open easily, as if it had been light as a feather.

However, the moment the door opened, we were blinded by a bright blue light. I shielded my eyes and then squinted at the source. It was too bright to look at directly, but slowly my eyes adjusted and I saw the light was emanating from a sword suspended in the air at the far side of the room. It was floating above a pedestal on a raised platform, and there were stairs leading up to it. Sparkling jewels were strewn about the floor and in piles all around the platform.

But it was the sword blade that consumed our attention. It wasn't just glowing, it was bordered by a blue flame that emitted a great deal of light. In fact, the sword was the only source of light in the room, bright enough to create long shadows behind us.

"Whoa!" Demetri said. "I would love to learn their smithing lore."

"It's so bright." Olivia said.

"And there is a fortune in precious gems in here." I said.

"No, these aren't precious gems." Sierra said, picking one up. "They are just broken bits of crystal." She was right. There were thousands of crystal fragments on the floor that ranged from the size of gravel up to about the size of my fist.

Lokir was staring at the sword transfixed. "I have no words…" he said (but none of us believed him). "It is a thing of fierce beauty—like the best aspects of a beautiful woman and the glory of war combined into a single object—I must have it!"

Lokir began striding resolutely toward it.

"Wait, Lokir!" I shouted, and my voice echoed in the chamber. He stopped, puzzled. Then I turned to Sierra. "The sword is dangerous, isn't it? This is the object the Dwarves made that destroyed them!"

"Yes, in a sense." Sierra said. "They made this sword, and as a result they were exterminated...by the Vampires."

"What? Why would the Vampires wipe out an entire race for making a sword?" Olivia asked.

"Because that blade is the only weapon ever made that could destroy the medallions." Sierra said. "And the ancient Vampire king made sure it would never be used."

"By killing everyone?" I asked. "Why didn't he just destroy the sword? That doesn't make sense. Why kill everyone?"

"Because that blade is indestructible!" Lokir shouted, and then I realized he was already halfway up the stairs to the pedestal. "Whoever wields this blade will never know defeat in battle!"

"Lokir, stop!!" Sierra rushed forward, sprinting faster than I thought she could move, and we all realized that Lokir must be in great danger, so we ran toward him also. But he heard us coming and ran up the last few steps before we could reach him.

Sierra was pleading. "No, Lokir! Don't touch it! It will kill—"

"I MUST HAVE IT!" Lokir shouted as he reached forward and grabbed the sword by the hilt.

We were too late. Lokir's hand was suddenly engulfed in blue flames, which quickly spread over his whole body. We stopped and watched in helpless horror as Lokir screamed in agony. His limbs went rigid and his flesh began to fall off in chunks as the flames ravaged his body. He released the sword and then toppled backward, still engulfed in blue flames, but when his body hit the stone steps he shattered like a mirror into a thousand pieces. We shielded our faces from the flying shards, and the sound of the crash echoed on the chamber's walls for a long time.

When there was finally silence again, we were all shocked, and Sierra was furious. "I tried to get him to stop!"

I looked down at one of the pieces of what used to be Lokir, and saw that it looked like a shattered piece of blue crystal. It wasn't flaming anymore, but I had no desire to touch it.

"Well, um...we tried." I said lamely. "Time to go home."

"No!" Sierra said. "Lokir was a fool and never should have tried to touch that sword."

"Right, and neither should we, so the quest is over!" Demetri said.

"I'm with you guys. Let's get out of here." Olivia said.

"Wait!" Sierra shouted. "We can't give up! Don't you understand what will happen if we don't get that sword? My parents will kill everyone! They'll never stop and the whole world will be empty just like this kingdom."

"Then we're all doomed, because there is nothing we can do." I said. "You saw what just happened to Lokir." Sierra approached me, reached out and took my hand. "Septimus, I think you're the only one who can get the sword."

"What? Why would you think that?" I asked.

"The amulet itself gave the clue to how it has to be done. This is why I went to find you. This is why Julius Aurelius wanted me to bring you to him, and why he wanted me to bring you here." Sierra said.

"Because the amulet mentions me?" I asked.

"Yes. There is a curse engraved right on the amulet that is directed at the seventh son of the Elven king of the Kingdom of the Sky. It is the inverse of the runespell engraved on the pedestal. *Drocnod*, the blade of the blue flame, can only be removed from this chamber by the seventh son of the Elven king of the Kingdom of the Sky."

"Why would the Dwarves do that?" I asked.

"Because they were being destroyed by the Vampires and their own astrologers and stargazers predicted their doom, but they found a way to reverse the Vampires' victories at a distant point in the future. It was supposed to be accomplished with this sword." Sierra explained.

"They knew the Vampires had the power to destroy the race of Dwarves and erase their memory from the kingdoms of the world, so the Dwarves made certain they could not destroy this. The Dwarves combined all of their lore and all of the magic of their wizards to form a spell of protection that would last through the ages, and provide a chance for revenge from beyond the grave."

"This sword will do that?" I asked.

"The protective spell will destroy anyone who tries to touch the sword—except for you." Sierra said. "I believe that you were born to wield that sword, to avenge the Dwarves and stop the destruction of the world. You just need to go and take it."

I nodded. If Sierra was right about what her parents were planning, it was only a matter of time before they killed everyone anyway. I might as well do something heroic to try to stop them.

I took a deep breath and walked up the stairs, cringing as my boots crunched on the broken crystals under my feet. I got nearly to the top and froze. Could I make myself do this? I might only be seconds away from the fate that Lokir just suffered.

"Sierra?" I said, my voice shaking a little. "Are you sure about this?"

Sierra was at my side a moment later and she grabbed my chin and pulled my face toward her. "I would never ask you to do this if I didn't think you could do it." Then she put her arms around me and kissed me. A rush of relief and adrenalin washed over me at the same time, and then I relaxed and kissed her back.

Sierra pulled away, smiling. "You were meant to take *Drocnod*. It is your fate."

"That sounds both encouraging and scary at the same time." I said. There was no point in fighting it. I had to try to get the sword. "I'm doing this for the good of all of the races of the world...and not just because you kissed me!"

I walked right up to the pedestal and faced the glowing blue sword. Standing this close I could see that it was made of some strange black metal that I had never seen before. Blue runes were engraved on the blade, so it seemed that the flame was coming from within the metal.

I took a deep breath and grabbed the hilt. It was freezing cold. That surprised me, but I noticed that the flames weren't spreading up my arm. I pulled on the sword and it felt like I was pulling apart two great magnets as I tried to wrestle it from the magical force field of the pedestal. I pulled harder and the sword seemed to fight me for a moment, then popped out of its place in the air. As soon as it left the magical force field, the flame went out, and amazingly—a sheath grew around the blade.

I examined it for a moment, then drew the sword from the new sheath. When I did so, the blade caught fire again. I turned to face my friends and realized they were already cheering.

I came back down from the platform (almost slipping on the shards of Lokir), and displayed the flaming sword to the others, who were both amazed and a little scared.

"Is it safe if I hold it?" Demetri asked.

"Are you sure you want to find out?"

"Demetri, it should be totally fine." Sierra said. "The spell was on the pedestal, not on the sword itself." Then Sierra added. "I'm pretty sure."

Demetri looked at her uncertainly, then made a decision and reached for the hilt. I handed it to him, and immediately after it left my hand the flame went out.

"What? What happened?" Demetri asked.

"Let me see." I said.

As soon as I touched the sword it caught fire again.

"Looks like it only works if Septimus is holding it." Olivia said.

I sheathed the sword and then removed my old sword from my belt and handed it to Demetri.

"What am I supposed to do with this?" He asked.

"I don't know. You're a blacksmith—I'm sure you'll figure out something."

I hung the new sheath onto my belt and patted it. "So, you think it's time to get out of here?"

"It's time." Sierra chuckled.

We descended the endless flight of stairs, made our way across the long walkway, and then walked out the front doors into the bright sunlight.

When we got outside guess who was waiting for us? You guessed it...it was the ugly bandit Victor and his henchmen! (Or maybe you didn't guess it).

"Allo Septimus, Demetri...Vampire girl, we meet again!" Then Victor looked at Olivia. "Ooh, and who's this, ay? Another beautiful lass joining Septimus Legion's adventure?

"That's my cousin, Olivia, and you will leave her alone." I said.

"I don't think you're in a position to make any demands. But uh, where is the other lad who went in there with you? Hmm?"

"He didn't make it." I said.

"Oh, made an earth-shattering discovery, did he?" Victor chuckled. "Maybe touched a blue sword when it had that awful curse on it?"

"How would you know that?" I asked.

"I've been here before." Victor snapped.

That surprised me. How could Victor have known about this place? Why would he come here? Then it dawned on me. "Did you know Julius Aurelius?" I asked.

"Ha! I followed the foolish scholar here once. He was following clues, making a map...and then I caught him and held him for ransom."

"And you found the cursed sword."

"Aye! But I lost three of my men before we realized that we couldn't break the curse. You see? You're not the first one to try to get the sword."

"But it looks like he's the only successful one." Olivia said.

Victor gave her a dirty look. "Yes well, we're very glad of that, because we'll be taking that sword now." Victor strode forward and placed the point of his drawn sword on my throat. "And you'll be coming with us until we receive a ransom paid by your father."

"Wait Victor, you don't know what you're doing!" Sierra said.

"Sure I do! I'm about to take that sword from Septimus and sell it for a small fortune." Victor said. "And I'm going to add to that fortune by holding all of you for ransom."

"But that money won't do you any good when the Vampires attack and you die with it." Demetri said.

"What are you talking about?"

"They're telling the truth." Olivia said. "There is a terrible war coming, and none of us will survive unless we use the sword to stop it. This is the only way to prevent a Vampire apocalypse."

That gave me an idea. "So instead of robbing us, why don't you join us and help us defeat the Vampires? Assuming we all survive you could gain an even bigger fortune...and be able to enjoy it."

"Or, I could take the sword and stop the Vampires myself. Then I could have all of the plunder for myself, and still hold you hostage."

"Well there are two problems with that idea." I said, thinking quickly. "First, you are going to need an enormous army to defeat the Vampires. And second, I'm the only one who can do this…" I drew *Drocnod* from its sheath and it burst in blue flame, the runes on the dark blade burned a bright blue.

"He's the only one who can make it do that." Sierra said. "And it if it doesn't do that, then there is no way to stop the Vampires."

"Hmm," Victor said, I could see the wheels turning in his mind, and I carefully sheathed *Drocnod*. "You're not too good with a sword, lad, but you are talented with words. Alright, we will help you...for the money." He finally lowered his sword and I breathed a sigh of relief. "But where were you planning to get an army big enough to defeat the Vampires?"

"The Elves of the Kingdom of the Sky have a huge army. My father will send troops." I said.

"Only if he believes you." Victor said. "And even if he does, we'll be needing more than that. The Vampires have the largest army of any kingdom."

"We can send a message to King Helios to see if he will send troops from The Kingdom of the Sun." Demetri suggested.

Sierra shook her head. "King Helios is insane, and has already tried to kill us. He's going to be even less reasonable when he finds out that Prince Lokir is dead."

"Then it will just be the army of the Elves against the army of the Vampires, even if they outnumber us." Olivia said.

Victor sighed. "It sounds like I will have to call in a favor. There is an Orc general I know who hates Vampires and owes me a wee debt. Get on your horses kids, we're going to pay him a visit."

Chapter Twelve: Building an Army

None of us were excited about visiting an Orc general, or visiting any Orcs at all, for that matter. We had all been raised on tales of Orc savagery and ruthlessness, but Victor assured us that there was more than one kind of Orc.

It took us a week to ride back out of the barren wastes, traveling Northeast towards the frontier between the Orc and Vampire lands, and then two more weeks to ride around the mountains and avoid most of the Orc settlements. The Orc camp we were heading to was apparently on the border with the Vampire kingdom.

We smelled the Orc camp almost as soon as we saw it, and the stench was awful. The camp was a small city of wood frame tents covered with hides, and the city was surrounded by a wall of logs with a tall stone tower in the middle of the camp.

We didn't receive a warm welcome. Orc scouts spotted us when we were far off, but Victor had produced a square of black cloth with a red symbol in the shape of a skull, which he attached to a stick and held it aloft like a flag as we approached. The Orcs apparently recognized it and didn't attack us, but they still looked wary of us. Orcs were on the walls surrounding the camp and watched us with bows drawn as we approached the timber gate.

"Halt!" One of the Orcs said in a deep, grating voice.

"Identify yourself and explain your intrusion!"

"I bear the colors of General Bruk-rot." Victor said.

"I can see what you're holding, and that wasn't my question!" The Orc roared. "Now this is your last chance to tell me your name, worm, or I'll throttle you with that flag and we'll all have an early dinner!" All the Orcs laughed and roared at that comment.

"My apologies! Yes, of course, my name. Um, I am Victor, the notorious bandit of the East. I am traveling with my loyal men, and with a few Elves that I have taken hostage. I have come to speak with General Bruk-rot about a very important matter." Victor said. "Now if you'll be so kind...please inform General Bruk-rot that I am here."

The Orc guard glared at Victor and then at us for a moment, then turned and spoke to the other Orc guards in the Orc language, which sounded like a lot of grunting, growling, and gagging. There seemed to be a bit of an argument going on, or maybe that's just the way they talked, but eventually the guard turned back to us.

"Get off your horses." The Orc guard said gruffly. "You are permitted to enter."

We reluctantly dismounted and led our horses as the gate opened, and we were ushered inside by a dozen guards who surrounded us. I was extremely nervous about this at first, but then realized they were escorting us through the camp, and soon felt relieved that they were there.

Hundreds of Orcs were milling around in the Orc city. There was a lot of chaos with Orcs shouting, arguing, clanging metal, and even fighting, but the guards around us kept the hordes away. We also saw Orcs working, butchering animals, cooking, and engaged in other activities, and they all stopped to stare at us as we passed.

We were led through a random maze of tents and crude wooden structures to the base of the stone tower where they had erected a throne made of animal bones. On the throne sat the largest Orc I had ever seen.

The Orc from the gate approached the great Orc sitting on the throne. "General Bruk-rot, there is a worm of a Man who calls himself Victor Bandit. I would have killed him at the gate, but he has your emblem. He says he wants to speak with you."

Bruk-rot peered at Victor through narrowed eyes, and then grunted.

"Leave us!" Bruk-rot's voice was deep, and he looked fierce. He wore black armor splattered red with what appeared to be the blood of Men or Elves. He had piercing yellow eyes, and I guessed he must have been at least seven feet tall, although it was hard to tell while he was seated on his throne. He had a black goatee which contrasted with his pale and blotchy skin, and he was as bald as Victor (but twice as ugly, if that's even possible).

"Ah, Bruk-rot, it's good to see you!' Victor said.

"Why are you here?" Bruk-rot growled.

"Yes, I will get right to the point. I've come here to use that wee favor you owe me."

"And who are they?" Bruk-rot grunted, pointing at us. "I don't owe anything to them."

"Oh, um, we have Demetri Smith, uh…Olivia Legion, Sierra Evans, and Septimus Legion." Victor said while pointing at each of us when he said our names.

Suddenly Bruk-rot's eyes turned all black for a minute or two then turned back to normal.

"Aracnash wants to see those two in private." Bruk-rot pointed at me and Sierra. "He is waiting in the top of the tower. Send them up now."

We all looked up at the stone tower, which was extremely high, but didn't appear to be completely stable.

"Up there? Okay...um, Septimus, Sierra, he wants you to go to the top of the tower." Victor said.

We had no choice. We walked into the tower, and climbed the many crooked, winding stairs past several platforms to the top of the tower. At the top of the tower we emerged into a room crammed with bookshelves filled with thousands of books. I never would have expected that in an Orc camp. I was looking around at all the books for a few moments before I realized that there was a shriveled old Orc sitting cross-legged on the floor, reading a book.

"Oh, hello," I said, but he didn't respond. I looked at Sierra and we waited for a few moments in silence, then I spoke again. "Excuse me, did you want to see us?"

The old Orc didn't seem to hear us, but was very interested in whatever it was he was reading. He turned the page and continued for a few more moments and then grunted and snapped the book closed.

He squinted up at us, then rose to his feet and jammed the book onto a crowded shelf. "Ah! Prince Septimus Legion and Princess Sierra Evans! It is an honor." The old Orc then bowed to us, which was even more shocking than seeing him read a book.

"Are you Aracnash?" Sierra asked.

"Yes, I am indeed! Wizard of the West, leader of the Krumpatosh Orcs." Aracnash said. He looked extremely old, but unlike any Orc I had seen so far. His pale skin was wrinkly and sagging from his bones like wet clothes. He had long white hair, drooping pointed ears, a long white beard, and he wore red robes. He looked so old that I suspected it must be magic that was keeping him alive, yet his brown eyes were sharp.

I glanced at his pointed ears again, and it suddenly hit me. "Wait, you're not an Orc...you're an Elf!"

Aracnash found this funny because he let out a wheezing laugh that quickly turned into a coughing fit. When he recovered he grinned at me. "Yes, I am indeed!"

"But you're the leader of the Orcs?" Sierra asked.

"Yes, well not the leader of all Orcs, just this city. Did you know that there were once nine factions? They have battled each other for dominance over the centuries, and now there are only five Orc factions that remain." Aracnash said. "I lead just one faction, the Krumpatosh Orcs, and we guard the border with the Vampires and keep an eye on them."

"So, why did you want to see us?" I asked.

"Because I know why you are here." Aracnash said. "I know much and I see far, Septimus Legion. You have obtained the ancient sword *Drocnod,* and now you need to build an army to fight the Vampires."

Aracnash turned to Sierra. "And would you really join that battle against your own parents, Sierra Evans?"

"Yes, of course! I'm the one who started this quest." Sierra said defensively. "I'm the one who found Septimus and told him that we needed to stop my parents before they destroyed the whole world. Of course I would join the battle against my parents!"

Aracnash peered at Sierra with his piercing brown eyes for a long moment, then smiled faintly and nodded.

He faced me again. "You will need a great army if you want to attack the Vampire forces in their own lands, before they begin their campaign of terror. You don't have much time. Have you already contacted your father to assemble the Elven army and start their march?"

"Not yet. I was—"

"What are you waiting for?" Aracnash snapped. "That will take time!"

"I'm not waiting for anything, I just haven't had a chance. We came straight here from the Dwarf kingdom with *Drocnod.*" I explained. "But it will take several weeks to send a messenger to my father, and I just hope he'll listen and take action..."

"I see the predicament you are in." Aracnash sighed. "Not to worry, I can help. Write a message in your own hand, and I have a way to deliver it to your father tonight. However, that is only the first step."

"I know. We need a bigger army." I said.

"Yes, and if you ask you shall have one. I am willing to send General Bruk-rot and the army of the Krumpatosh Orcs on such an important task; but tell me Septimus, do you think that this is the best decision?" Aracnash asked.

I was confused. "Yes? I mean, yes, of course! But why do you ask?"

"Because you haven't considered the cost yet." Aracnash said. "My help will come at a price."

"Yeah, well the whole world will be destroyed if we don't succeed here." I said. "So how much do you want?"

"No, you don't understand. I don't want money."

"What do you want then? Treasure? Power? A kiss from my cousin Olivia? Like I said, the whole world is going to be destroyed if we fail, so pretty much everything is on the table. What do you want?"

"I want you to give me the amulets—or what is left of them after you've destroyed them, obviously." Aracnash said. I looked at Sierra and she shrugged.

"Sure, why not?" I said.

"Excellent! Then we have a deal. I'm certain that we will win this war, all of the kingdoms will be preserved, and you will get me those amulets." Aracnash said.

I was glad he was optimistic because it all seemed like a longshot to me.

He provided me with parchment, ink, and a quill so that I could write a letter to my father explaining as simply as possible what was going on and what we needed. I signed it and gave it to Aracnash, who again assured me that my father would receive the message tonight. Then Sierra and I left the tower and told Victor and the others the good news.

Bruk-rot arranged for a clearing to be made near the tower where we set up our own little camp, which was still guarded by a dozen Orcs who kept away any Orc that might want to stir up trouble. That night it rained hard and the thunder shook the ground, but our borrowed Orc tents kept us dry (even if they were awfully smelly).

The next morning the rain had stopped but it was still dark and overcast, and I was shivering beside a smoky fire, sitting next to Victor. I could tell he had done some thinking the night before.

"Alright lad, I just have one wee problem with all of this." Victor said.

"And that is?" I asked.

"That you're planning to fight the most powerful beings in this world, and you're not prepared."

"We've been preparing ever since we got the sword." I said.

"Have you really?" Victor said. "So you're not terrible at sword fighting anymore?"

"Hey, I've been in a real battle and made it out alive. Not everyone can say that."

"You're right, they can't. Your horse also made it out of a real battle alive, and he can't say it because he's a horse. And you're about as good at sword fighting as he is."

"So? What are you going to do about it?" I asked.

"I'm gonna train you for the next three weeks." Victor said. "Because if I don't, then you're going to fail and we'll all be dead. And I'll never get my small fortune, let alone have a chance to enjoy it."

"Three weeks?"

"Yes. I know that's not a lot of time, but we're only going to focus on a few maneuvers and hitting a swinging metal object. Even you should be able to learn that in three weeks."

"Hey, I'll have you know that I had lessons as a child, and I wasn't the worst in the class. Usually."

"Actually, we have four weeks." Victor said.

"Four? How do we have four weeks?" I asked

"It will take your father's army three weeks to arrive, but you can bet it will take another week for the generals to put together a plan they can agree on. So four weeks of training."

"You think I'll be good enough to stand a chance against the Vampires?"

"I don't know about that. I'm just going to make sure you're skilled enough not to accidentally kill yourself with your sword when you see the Vampires." Victor said.

"Ha ha ha. So when does this training start?" I asked.

"Right now!" Victor said, suddenly leaping to his feet and drawing his sword in a single motion.

I jumped up to draw my sword and stepped in a puddle, splashing water and mud on both of us.

"Not bad!" Victor said, wiping mud out of his eye. "Take advantage of everything around you. If you want to win, then your weapon of victory is not just the sword in your hand, it is everything around you. Now raise your guard or I will smack the side of your face with the flat of my blade."

He smacked my face over and over. I started getting better at raising my guard and keeping my eyes directed at his chest (so he couldn't misdirect me with his eyes), but he gave me one sound beating after another.

Demetri and Sierra practiced, too, while Olivia practiced archery (and won several contests against Orc bowmen), but none of them were as physically exhausted at the end of the day as I was. And that was just the first day.

Every morning Victor would wake me up to take me to the training grounds, and he would teach me defensive techniques and then give me a beating as I failed again and again. We would train footwork, dodging, blocks, parries, and other defenses until midday, then take a break to rest and have some lunch. Afterward it was back to training.

In the afternoons he would teach me offensive techniques; jabs, swipes, slashes, with one hand and with two hands, and then he would test me—and easily defend against my best attempts (which was probably good for him, because I was attacking with a flaming sword).

We would stop again to rest and enjoy an evening meal, then he would take a long pole with a piece of rope tied to the end, and dangle a tin cup from the end of the rope.

My job was to cut the cup in half, but he would jerk it out of the way before I could even touch it with my sword, and I spent all evening swinging my sword through the air, always missing the cup until my arms, back, and shoulders were so sore that I couldn't lift the sword anymore. When it was too dark to see, I would finally stagger back to my tent and collapse into a deep sleep until morning.

By the middle of the first week I had sustained enough injuries to make me feel like I had already fought a battle. I had a pulled muscle in my shoulder, a twisted ankle, bruises everywhere, and several deep cuts that required the help of an Orc healer who had a little experience treating Elves. His skill wasn't nearly as good as Philo's had been in the Kingdom of the Sun, but it was good enough that I could continue training. By the middle of the second week I was not only worn out, I was sick of the stupid training and wanted to give up.

"Come on, Septimus! Are you even trying?" Victor said, dodging my attack and kicking my foot out from under me, so I went crashing to the ground.

I rolled over on my side, moaning. My body was so sore I couldn't stand. There were new cuts and bruises from today, and I could taste blood in my mouth from when Victor punched me in the face.

"I really don't think this is training." I said weakly.

"I'm pretty sure you're just doing this to beat me up."

"Come on, laddy, this is an example of real battle!" Victor said, kicking me in the gut. "Now get up!"

"Septimus, Victor is right." Sierra said. She and Demetri had stopped their training to watch me. "If my parents don't kill you immediately, they will beat you until you are too weak to stand. If you stop defending yourself, they won't show you mercy or let you rest. They will just kill you."

"That's right!" Victor said, kicking me in the head. "Now defend yourself against my attacks whether you're standing or lying on the ground. Your opponent won't care a wee bit how tired you are!"

I heard what they were saying, but that second kick had done something, and I was too sore to move. My head was spinning and my thoughts were grim...I started thinking that maybe I should just let Victor kill me now and I wouldn't have to go through any more torture. I barely noticed that Victor had raised his sword above his head and was about to swing, but Sierra stepped forward deflected it with her sword.

"Stop!" Sierra said.

"Little lass, were in the middle of training!" Victor said.

"Yes, but look at him! You're literally killing him! Now back away!" Sierra said.

"Septimus, are you okay?" Demetri said, but his voice sounded far away, and I didn't feel like answering.

Sierra kneeled down next to me, and I felt her warmth. "Septimus, look at me. Look right here."

I looked up and saw a dark blur. What was I looking at? I closed my eyes and I could hear her talking. Sierra wanted me to look? I didn't want to look, I wanted to go to sleep. No, she is telling me to look, so maybe I should try?

I opened my eyes again and there was still a blur, but it was brighter. I tried to focus, and suddenly I realized that I was looking into Sierra's dazzling eyes and the fog in my mind dissipated.

"Septimus, are you okay? Can you stand if help you?" Sierra asked.

"Yes, I think so." I said weakly.

Sierra and Demetri helped me up and walked me to the healer's tent and sat me down on a crude stool. Sierra found bandages for my new cuts and got me some water to drink, while Demetri went to go find the Orc healer.

"How do you feel?" Sierra asked a few minutes later, after the Orc healer had done his work.

"A little worse for wear, but I'm okay, Sierra." I said weakly.

"You're not okay! Victor has turned you into a training dummy!" Sierra said.

"It's fine. Like you said, your parents aren't going to show me any mercy. I have to do this, and I think I'm getting better." I said.

"Actually, I think you're getting worse." Sierra said. "You should take a day off and let your body recover."

"No, I'm fine." I said getting up. "That Orc healer has fixed me up well enough that I can continue."

"No! You're done getting beaten up for today!" Sierra said.

She tried to stop me, but I got up and went back to the training grounds. Victor was leaning against a wooden training dummy, and it appeared that he had been waiting for me to return.

"Are you ready to start trying, now?" Victor said.

"Let's just get this over with." I said.

We drew our swords and I immediately lunged forward. My attack wasn't perfect, but I didn't slow down or give up. I kept pressing the attack while Victor dodged and blocked, and had to give up ground and take a few steps back.

"That's more like it!" Victor said.

He counter-attacked and I blocked his blows, but then he took a quick step forward and tried to punch me in the face. I dodged and I slammed my knee into his side. Victor fell to the ground, and I swung at him but he deflected my sword and jumped up and swung at me.

I blocked his attack and kicked him in the stomach knocking the breath out of him. He dropped to his knees, trying to catch his breath, but I didn't stop my attack. I swung at Victor and he blocked. I swung again, still Victor deflected. I swung again and again, beating down on his sword and then suddenly his sword broke in half, and my sword, glowing brighter than ever, sliced into his shoulder.

The Orcs watching our battle cheered at my victory. Sierra ran up to me and gave me a hug. "I can't believe it—you beat him!" Sierra said.

"That was much better," Victor winced, gripping the smoking, cauterized wound on his shoulder, but then he smiled. "I knew you had it in you. You're going to be ready, lad!"

I took Sierra's advice and rested the next day, but the following day we were at it again, and I could finally feel the progress I was making. I was getting better at attacks and defenses, and I was also able to hit the swinging cup from time to time.

Within a few days I had split the cup in half and we had to find other metal objects to swing from the rope at the end of the pole. I chopped through several of those, too. My sword was incredibly sharp and strong, and when I was focused it seemed that it could cut through anything.

At the end of the third week the Orc scouts reported that an army was approaching. I was certain that it was my father's army, led by my eldest brother Maximus, but I was wrong.

We climbed onto the rampart on the city wall to greet them. As they approached and began setting up their camp outside of the Orc city, we saw that it wasn't Elves at all. It was an army of Men under the banner of the Kingdom of the Sun, also carrying the emblem of General Bruk-rot.

"Where did they come from?" I asked.

"I invited them." Olivia said. "Sort of."

"How did you sort of invite them??" Demetri asked.

"I was speaking with Aracnash in the tower and told him about my friend, Philo, who lives in the Kingdom of the Sun. Aracnash asked me to send him a message, and see if he could convince any of the soldiers of Men to come fight the Vampires with us. I never heard back from Philo, but it looks like he was successful."

Later that afternoon we learned that he had only been partially successful. This group was just one battalion of the army of Men, led by a captain named Guntir. It turned out that Captain Guntir's father was an old friend of Philo's, and after a little persuasion by his father he had come with all of his men.

Captain Guntir was the only leader of Men who had been willing to heed the call to help the Orcs fight the Vampires. He had assembled his men and prepared to march, but was having trouble getting King Helios to give him provisions, so Philo emptied his larders and his storeroom in the tavern to help supply the battalion.

That wasn't the only army that arrived at the Orc camp that day. Just before nightfall the second army arrived, and this time it was the Elven army of the Kingdom of the Sky, led by my brother, General Maximus.

"Maximus!" I shouted, as I ran to greet him.
He laughed when he saw me, and jumped off his horse.
"Septimus! It's been a long time since I've seen you." Maximus said while giving me a hug. "What have you been up to?"

"So many adventures!" I said. "Look at this..." I drew *Drocnod* from its sheath, and it burst into blue flame.

Maximus wanted to hold it, but was disappointed when the flames instantly extinguished. Just then Olivia ran to him and gave him a hug as well.

"Olivia! What are you doing here, cousin!"

We spent the evening telling Maximus the tale of our adventures while we helped him set up his tent. His army camped on the other side of the army of Men, and he insisted on leaving some space so that they wouldn't feel crowded.

"How is Father?" I asked later, while we were eating dinner around a roaring fire in Maximus's camp.

"He's doing well, the whole family is well, and Henrik is still causing mischief." Maximus said.

"Of course he is! Hopefully he hasn't burned down the palace, though." I said.

"That's not for the lack of trying—"

Just then Victor jogged up to us. "Oy there, General Maximus! I've come to let you know that it's time to get the war council going! General Bruk-rot and Captain Guntir are waiting for you in the War Leaders tent near the tower. I'll lead the way." Victor said.

"Very well, are you coming Septimus?" Maximus asked.

"Not tonight. I have my own plans to make with Sierra. I'll see you a little later." I was tired, and there was no reason for me to be in the war council tonight. I wasn't going to be participating in the battle directly. Instead, I would be with Sierra deep behind the Vampire lines, and ours would be the most important mission of the war.

Chapter Thirteen: War

Three days later, Victor, Maximus, Guntir, and Bruk-rot had agreed on a plan, and today we would begin our march north into the Vampire lands. Early in the morning Victor summoned me, Sierra, Demetri, and Olivia to the war leader's tent. It was enormous—larger than a house—and it was covered in black skins, which made the inside look like the Orc's symbol, the night sky.

When we entered the tent, the first thing that caught our attention was a huge table with a map of the Vampire kingdom spread across it. On top of the map were colored cubes and miniature flags representing troops of the different armies. Several lieutenants and captains from each army were standing around that map table, or seated on stools around the other three tables in the room, drinking and talking.

The junior officers were dismissed as soon as we arrived. I could tell that some of them were a little miffed that they weren't allowed to stay. Once they had left, the room seemed much emptier. There were a few pieces of furniture, including a short bookshelf full of books, a wooden chest, and three crude tables with a dozen stools, around them. There was only one chair, which was so large that it could only have belonged to General Bruk-rot.

Victor and Bruk-rot were still leaning over the map table, while Maximus and Guntir were seated on stools, and Aracnash was sitting in Bruk-rot's giant chair. The chair was so large that I almost laughed because it made the shriveled little Elf, Aracnash, look like a small child. It was also surprising to see him here because he rarely came down from his tower.

Victor looked up at us. "As you can see, the armies of Orcs, Elves, and Men have worked out their strategies. Our spies have brought us news that the Vampire armies are gathering on the field in front of the city."

We looked at the map and noticed the red flags and cubes in front of the outline of the city. Blue, black, and yellow cubes and flags represented the armies of Elves, Orcs, and Men. There were more red cubes than all of the other colors combined.

"It looks like we're still outnumbered." I said.

"Our spies tell us that the Vampire king and queen have summoned all of the lords of the Vampire lands. They are bringing troops from every corner of the kingdom." Aracnash said.

"Yes, their numbers are already much greater than ours, and they are growing." Bruk-rot said. "We will need to attack soon."

"What is your plan?" Sierra asked.

Maximus looked grave. "We will carry out a three-pronged attack on the Vampire armies in front of the gates. If we can surprise them it will help, but we will lose a lot of soldiers no matter how this plays out. We must attack them on the field before they begin their march south, and hold them there until you have completed your secret mission."

"How long do you think you can hold them?" Olivia asked.

"Hours, perhaps." Captain Guntir said.

"The Elven army is the largest, so it will attack first from the front." Maximus said. "The two armies of Orcs and Men will remain hidden until after the fighting starts. Once the Vampires rush forward to meet the Elves, the Orcs and Men will emerge from the forest to the East and West and attack from the sides."

"Septimus and Sierra, these valiant men will engage the Vampire forces and keep them occupied while you sneak into the city to destroy the amulets." Aracnash said. "We in this tent are the only ones who know about your secret mission. Not even the officers know about it, so if they are caught they will not be able to reveal anything."

"Now, would you care to share your plan with us?" Victor asked. "And it had better be good!"

"It's pretty simple," Sierra said. "We're all going to dress in the Vampire armor the Orcs have collected, then sneak into the tallest tower of the castle. I've drawn a map of the layout of the castle and made the others memorize it, in case we are separated."

"You're sure your parents will be in the tower?" Maximus asked.

Sierra nodded. "I'm certain that's where they will be once the fighting starts—as long as you engage the Vampire army on the field in front of the city. The observatory with telescopes is in the tallest tower, and it has the best view. My parents enjoy watching battles." Sierra said.

"Don't we all?" Victor smirked. "Anyway, the Vampire armor is in these chests. Try it on and make sure it fits."

We tried on the various pieces of armor which consisted of chest plates, gauntlets, greaves (to protect our shins and feet), and open-faced helmets. The vampire armor was a dark ruby color, and was decorated with many moon emblems—for example, the shoulder pauldrons had crescent moons on them, and there was a full moon right in the middle of the chest plate. It didn't fit perfectly—Olivia's was too large and Demetri's was too small—but it was close enough.

"You guys don't look much like Vampire soldiers. Well, except for Sierra because she is one." Maximus smiled. "Maybe put your cloaks on with your hoods up? It will hide your faces and probably make you look more like Vampires."

We agreed that was a good idea, and dutifully put our cloaks on, with our hoods up over the helmets.

"There now! You all look like those blood-sucking beasts! Oh, sorry Sierra. No offense." Victor snickered.

"Don't worry about it." Sierra said. "It's what I would expect from a bald, scum-sucking slug like you. No offense, of course."

Victor scowled at her and put his hand on the hilt of his sword. It was tense for a moment, then Victor barked out a laugh and everyone chuckled and let out a sigh of relief.

"So what's your job, Victor?" Demetri asked.

"Oh, my men and I get the fun job! We'll be wearing Vampire armor, too! But we'll be sneaking around behind the enemy lines and wreaking havoc—setting fires, scattering horses, stabbing the enemy in the back—sabotage and savagery is our job!"

"It suits you." Sierra said.

"I have a job, too." Aracnash said. "I'm too old for war, so I'll be climbing the stairs up to my tower and taking a nap."

I believed him.

With preparations and plans in place, we struck camp and traveled for two days in drizzling rain with the armies of Orcs, Men, and Elves, watching out for Vampire scouts and receiving reports from our own spies as we went. Twice we spotted hidden Vampire scouts that were watching our movements from afar.

They probably thought they were out of range of our arrows, but each time Olivia took out her bow, took careful aim, and brought them down with a single arrow. They were clean shots that killed instantly. As far as we knew, we still had the element of surprise.

The three armies parted when they were a few miles away from the Vampire city. Now was the most critical time to avoid detection before we launched our attack. The Orc army went northeast, and the army of Men went northwest, while we remained with the Elven army that continued straight north. Olivia shot four more Vampires as we approached the city, and their bodies were retrieved and hidden.

When we were close enough to catch a glimpse of the city through the trees, I saw that it was built on a rocky island near the edge of a dark lake that stretched out far behind the city. The entrance to the city was a causeway with a drawbridge near the city gates, and the castle had five soaring towers. It was a formidable fortress, but the Vampire army wasn't inside the city; it was gathered on the field in front of the city, and their numbers were frightening. There had to be ten thousand of them.

The Elves gathered quietly, and as soon as the Elven army was in position, Maximus nodded to us. "It's time. We could be discovered any minute, which would start the battle prematurely. This is your chance. Go!"

We left the Elven army just inside the forest's edge and rode our horses across the muddy, soon-to-be battlefield toward the causeway and the drawbridge that would get us inside the city walls.

There were thousands of tents and Vampire troops on the field where they had been gathering for weeks, preparing for their assault on the lands to the South. The sky was dark and overcast with a light rain still coming down. Sierra rode in front, and we followed behind wearing our Vampire armor and hooded cloaks, making sure we kept our heads down.

Our disguises were sufficiently convincing to allow us to ride through the enormous encampment, right up the causeway, over the lowered drawbridge, and up to the city gates where we passed through without incident. We followed Sierra and dismounted when she did, then stabled our horses and followed her on foot to the castle.

We were halfway there when we heard horns sounding an alarm, and then explosions. We didn't know whether that was because of an attack by the Elven army or some kind of sabotage being carried out by Victor and his men.

Within minutes there was chaos all around as Vampire guards and soldiers rushed to the gates to defend the city. We continued to the castle unchallenged, but when we arrived we saw the front doors were being guarded by two tall vampire soldiers, both wielding war hammers.

"Halt! The horns have sounded! Why aren't you soldiers on the battlefield?" One of the guards asked.

"Uh...we are here to—" I said.

"Stand aside!" Sierra said, lowering her hood. "You know who I am."

"Princess Sierra! You've been gone so long." The guard said suspiciously.

"Too long," Sierra said. "An army of Elves is about to attack from the Southern forest. I've been among the enemy and I have important information for the king and queen. Now stand aside, or you'll suffer the wrath of the king."

The guards let us pass, and we entered the castle and found ourselves in the main throne room, which was empty. I recognized the layout of the room from the map Sierra had made us memorize, but she was here with us, so she led us through a doorway and down a hall to a flight of stairs.

This wasn't the shortest way to the observatory tower, but it was a way that would allow us to avoid the guards stationed inside the entrance at the bottom of the tower. If we entered through the doorway on the fourth floor, we hoped to be able to climb the stairs to the top without running into trouble.

We followed Sierra through corridors and up stairways to the fourth floor. We saw servants bustling around from time to time, but no one stopped us. Sierra led us through several hallways and then through the library to a door that led to the observatory tower. She opened the door and peeked inside, then motioned for us to follow quietly.

We snuck into the tower and began climbing as quietly as we could. We could hear the guards talking loudly several levels down. They were speculating on what was happening outside, and who would dare to attack the Vampires in their strongest city. We started our climb tiptoeing, but after several hundred steps our armor was feeling very heavy, and our footfalls grew louder and louder.

"Why are there so many stairs?" I asked.

"Yeah, I was already tired when we got to the library on the fourth floor—and now this!" Demetri said miserably.

"Come on, it's not going to kill you…" Olivia said breathlessly "...to walk up a few stairs!"

"It might kill Demetri." I chuckled. "His arms weigh as much as your whole body."

"Shush!" Sierra hissed. "Stop moaning and let's go! We are so close to completing our quest."

We trudged on, too winded to speak. Our feet thumped on the stairs, and our armor occasionally clanged into a wall, but nobody pursued us. It felt like hours walking up those stairs. When we finally reached the top we were all lightheaded and completely out of breath, and Demetri threw up.

Sierra was the only one who didn't look like she was about to black out. "We're here." She said, scowling at Demetri. Then started toward the door to the observatory, but I stopped her.

"Wait! Let's just take a moment to catch our breath, please!" I said. After we all caught our breath (and Demetri cleaned up his armor), Sierra opened the door and we went into the tower chamber.

Inside the observatory there were all kinds of brass instruments, many of them large telescopes. They looked a lot like some of the things we had seen in the Dwarf city, and I realized that they had probably been stolen by the ancient Vampire king when he destroyed the Dwarf civilization.

There were many windows in the walls, including one enormous window that looked out over the field in front of the city, but there were no guards in the room. Two huge thrones were situated in front of the window, each with a large, mounted telescope in front of it.

Sitting in those thrones were two people I realized must be Sierra's parents, the king and queen of the Kingdom of the Moon. Through the great window we could see the raging battle taking place on the battlefield.

I realized at once that something must have gone wrong with the three-pronged attack because the army of Men and the Elven army were fighting the Vampire army, and the army of the Orcs was rushing out of the forest to attack the exposed flank. The armies of the Orcs and Men were supposed to attack at the same time, and it looked like the army of Men was taking heavy losses. But there was nothing we could do to help them now—except complete our mission.

The king and queen were aware of us, but they did not seem at all concerned. They slowly rose from their thrones and looked at us curiously, then approached us with complete serenity.

I was not feeling calm at all. The king and queen were at least ten feet tall—they were like giants! They looked nothing like Sierra. Their fangs went down to their chins, and their golden amulets glinted on chains hanging in front of their chests.

The king had completely red eyes, short black hair (hidden inside his solid gold crown), and he wore his elaborate black and gold kingly robes. The queen also had red eyes and long black hair. Her black and gold robes were more elegant, and she had a solid gold tiara sitting on top of her head.

"Uninvited visitors, on a day like today?" The king asked. "Just like the uninvited, hostile troops our spies warned about."

Sierra removed her helmet and shook out her long brown hair.

"Ah, daughter! You have finally returned. Who have you brought with you?" The king asked.

"Have you come to watch the amusing battle with us?" The queen asked. "A ragtag group of Elves, Orcs, and Men are attacking us here in our stronghold. Can you believe it?"

Sierra shrugged. "Hello, Mother and Father. I'm home and I brought some friends to meet you."

Olivia, Demetri, and I all removed our hoods, and I was petrified.

"Do your friends have names?" The king asked.

It felt like my tongue was swelling in my mouth, but I still managed to say: "I am Septimus Legion, prince of the Kingdom of the Sky."

"The Kingdom of the Sky? Well, those are your people out there. What are you all doing here, in such a dangerous place, so far from home?" The queen asked calmly.

"I am here to stop you and put an end to your tyranny!" I said, wanting to sound brave, but my voice cracked at just the wrong moment.

"More amusement!" The queen laughed. "A little guy like you? Why, that's adorable!"

"Listen closely, Septimus Legion. You and your friends are children." The king was not laughing. "You don't know what you're doing. Now turn around and go back to your kingdom before you get hurt."

"Who's going to get hurt?" I asked shakily as I drew my sword. The king and queen backed away in surprise, staring at the black blade with the glowing blue flames.

"How dare you bring that filthy thing into our presence?!" The king spat.

"Oh, so you know this sword?" I asked, starting to feel more confident.

"Of course I know it! That blade is the cursed *Drocnod*..." The king said. "How did you get it?"

"You know the legend, Father—it is destined to destroy your precious amulets." Sierra said.

"You fools!" The queen hissed. "Don't you understand that these amulets are all that is preventing the world from falling into anarchy?"

"Is that the lie you tell your subjects?" Olivia asked.

"Enough of this! All of you will regret your insolence." The king said, drawing his greatsword.

"How can I regret insolence when I don't know what it is?" Demetri asked.

"Sierra," the queen said, shaking her head sadly. "Your friends obviously don't know you like we do, but don't you feel even a little bit of guilt about bringing them to their deaths? Because of you, their blood will soon be flowing onto my beautiful marble floor." She drew two long swords.

Olivia, Demetri, and Sierra also drew their weapons.

"Stop!" I shouted as the blade quivered in my hands. "This sword was created to destroy the amulets. Give them to me and let me destroy them. Nobody needs to get hurt."

"It doesn't matter what that cursed blade was created for!" The king snarled. "It will take more than a cursed sword in the hands of a mere boy to destroy the peace of our kingdom!"

We all just stood there glaring at each other, waiting for someone to make the first move.

Suddenly Demetri lunged and swiped at the king with his sword, but the queen's swords flashed in front of him and deflected his sword away with a clang. The king roared and swung his heavy sword at *Drocnod* and I blocked and stumbled back, knocking over a telescope. I was afraid his blow would drive me to the ground, but thankfully Sierra raised her sword and blocked at the same time, helping me deflect the king's powerful blow.

Meanwhile, Olivia drew her bow and shot straight at the queen, but when the arrow struck her it shattered into a thousand splinters and fell at her feet.

"Now you see the power of the amulet!" The queen said. "It's going to take more than that to defeat me!"

"Oh, yeah?" Demetri said as he lunged forward, swinging his sword toward the queen's face with one hand. She easily deflected his blow, but not before he grasped her amulet with his free hand and ripped it from the queen's neck.

"No!" The queen screamed and struck Demetri in the head with the hilts of both swords, knocking him to the floor unconscious. The amulet flew out of his hand as his body hit the smooth marble, and the amulet skidded toward me and struck my foot.

"Septimus, destroy it!" Sierra shouted.

I wanted to destroy it, but at that moment I had to leap out of the way, dodging a fierce attack from the king. He lunged again and I spun around, ducking under his sword and swung *Drocnod* at the amulet that was near the king's feet. When the black blade struck the amulet, there was a loud bang as the amulet shattered into large golden shards.

I staggered backward from the force of the blast and watched in horror as the queen raised both swords. She was poised over Demetri's unconscious body ready to plunge the blades into his chest.

But just then Olivia fired a volley of arrows in rapid succession, each one thudding as it pierced the queen's torso. She gurgled and fell to the ground next to Demetri in a heap. Blood oozed onto the marble floor as she lay still and lifeless.

"No!" The king yelled in agonized rage. He swung at me so powerfully that when I blocked it, the force of the blow sent me flying across the room. I slammed into one of the larger telescopes, knocking it through the giant glass window which shattered.

The heavy brass instrument fell out of the tower and I was showered with broken glass. I covered my face, and thankfully my armor protected me from the flying glass splinters.

When I looked up I saw the king rushing toward Olivia, determined to avenge the death of his wife, but Sierra jabbed her sword between his legs and he crashed to the floor. Her blade snapped at the hilt, but the king leapt to his feet unharmed.

"Sierra, stay out of this!" The king yelled.

I staggered to my feet and jogged toward him as he pursued Olivia who was weaving between the giant telescopes and ducking behind the thrones. The king swung his greatsword into the queen's throne, and it cracked in half and crumbled in front of him. Olivia screamed as the king swung again, but I jumped in front of her and wildly deflected the king's vicious blow with *Drocnod*.

"Leave her alone! This is your fault!" I shouted. He swung at me and my training took over. I blocked, then counterattacked, swinging *Drocnod* hard. My blazing sword was within inches of the swinging amulet hanging from his neck, but he blocked so hard that I lost my grip and *Drocnod* flew from hand. It hit the floor and the blue flames extinguished.

"Now you will die!" He said triumphantly.

I had his full attention and he wasn't attacking Olivia, but I didn't have my sword! I grabbed a brass instrument the size of my fist and threw it at his head, then dove for my sword, rolling and sliding across the slick marble floor.

Meanwhile Olivia fired several arrows at him that had no effect other than to distract him while I grabbed my black sword again. As soon as my finger touched the hilt, *Drocnod's* flames ignited and the runes glowed blue on the blade.

The king roared and took two great steps toward me as I jumped to my feet. He swung his enormous sword again and again, driving me back across the glass shards on the marble floor, toward the great broken window that overlooked the battlefield.

I blocked with all my strength, and *Drocnod* clanged and spat blue flame with each blow. My hands and arms were getting tired quickly—they were sore and rattled all the way up to my shoulders, and I felt myself weakening as he beat down on my sword.

I stumbled onto one knee, and suddenly imagined him shoving me out the broken window, sending me plummeting to my death from the soaring tower. No! I would not give up! I would not let that happen!

As he swung his greatsword again, I stepped aside and shoved a telescope, which swung around on its swivel base toward him. His sword cut right through the telescope, splitting it in two, and the pieces crashed to the ground. But that gave me a chance to get close to the amulet again. I swung hard, aiming right for the amulet, but he was too fast and blocked *Drocnod*, locking our swords at the hilt.

The king glared down at me, his eyes full of pain and fury. "What have you done?? You fools have murdered my wife! And now you want to plunge the world into anarchy!"

"Your wife was trying to kill my friend! If you had given me the amulets, nobody would have been hurt." I grunted, straining at the effort to keep his sword locked with mine.

"You don't understand. The fate of our world rests in your hands!" The king said.

"That's right, and I'm stopping your reign of terror!" I said.

"No, you will die to maintain balance in our world!"

The king ripped his sword free from mine and suddenly I saw Sierra behind him. She jumped and grabbed both of his arms from behind, and I saw my chance.

I thrust the blue flaming *Drocnod* through the amulet, and right into his chest. His amulet cracked with a loud bang, and then fell from his neck in pieces.

There was a rushing sound and Sierra tumbled to the floor, and the king dropped to his knees with the black blade through his heart.

"You…you have chosen Doom…" The king whispered with his dying breath. I pulled the sword free and his enormous body crumpled to the floor.

Sierra slowly rose to her feet. "My power is back!" She said, smiling at me with tears in her eyes and gave me a huge hug. "I can feel it!"

I noticed then that Olivia was helping Demetri to his feet, and he was rubbing his head.

"Did we do it? Did we win?" Demetri asked.

"We won." Sierra laughed, tears streaming down her face.

Epilogue

The war ended as soon as the second amulet was destroyed. All of the Vampires fell to the ground when their power was restored and the fighting stopped almost immediately. The Elves, Orcs and Men recognized what had happened, sounded a retreat on their war horns, and withdrew from the Vampires back to the forest.

The Vampires quickly realized that they were no longer forced to obey a tyrant of a king, and retreated from the field back to the city. Some of them began transforming into bats for the first time in their lives and soared into the sky. (By the way, I gave Sierra a hug to try to comfort her and she kissed me—for real this time—but that's all I have to say about that, because come on, this isn't a kissing book)!

Shortly afterward, Sierra met with the generals, lords, and nobles of the Vampires. Once they understood that she had freed them from her parents' cruelty, they acclaimed her as the new queen of the Vampire kingdom. Meanwhile, I had not forgotten my promise, and I gathered the golden shards of the amulets to deliver to Aracnash.

Soon healers were out on the field tending to the wounded, and soldiers were tending to the corpses of their fallen comrades. We learned with sadness that both Victor and Captain Guntir had been slain in battle. The army of Men had been discovered too soon and they were attacked first. The explosions we heard at the beginning of the battle were from the Knights of Men, but many of them had fallen before the Elven and Orc armies came to their rescue.

Victor and his men had gotten themselves trapped behind enemy lines and most of them perished as well. The three-pronged attack didn't work out as planned, but thankfully the sacrifices made by the brave warriors were effective—they had kept the Vampire army occupied while we carried out our mission in the tower to destroy the amulets.

The day after Sierra was crowned queen of the Vampires, many of the Vampire lords and nobles returned to their own regions with their armies. Now that the war was over, Sierra invited Demetri, Olivia, Maximus, Bruk-rot, and me to the throne room to discuss our plans.

"You are welcome to stay as long as you like." Sierra said. "I've made arrangements for all of you to be housed here in my castle until you are ready to return to your homes."

"Very kind, but I've had about enough of this castle." Demetri said, rubbing his head. Sierra was wearing the solid gold tiara of the queen, while Demetri was wearing a bandage over his head from the wound he received from the former queen.

"I suppose that is understandable." Sierra smiled. "What about the rest of you?"

"Your offer is kind, but my soldiers and I will be leaving soon." Maximus said. "My men are anxious to return to their families, and we must return the ashes of our fallen soldiers to their kin."

"You will take them more than that." Sierra said. "The noble sacrifices of those soldiers have saved us all, and I want to seal our peace with good will. I have decreed that every soldier who fought for freedom will receive a reward from my treasury, and every soldier who perished will receive a triple reward to be given to his family. Instead of war we will have peace, prosperity, and trade with our neighbors."

"You are going to make a wonderful queen of the Vampires." Olivia said.

"Your generosity will win the favor of many Orcs." Bruk-rot said. "We are leaving today, but I will gladly take treasure back to my people."

"You can also take the amulet shards." I said, handing him a leather pouch. "I can trust you to give them to Aracnash?"

"Of course! Orcs are honorable. And I have learned that some Elves, Men, and even Vampires are honorable as well."

"So, wait—who all is staying here in the castle?" I asked. "Just me and Olivia?"

"Actually Septimus...Demetri and I are both leaving with Maximus today." Olivia said.

"What? Why leave so soon?"

"I'm not looking forward to another long journey, but I miss my home." Olivia said.

"I can understand that." I nodded.

"It sounds like it's just you, Septimus. You are staying, aren't you?" Sierra asked.

"Yes, I'll hang around here—for a while anyway." I said.

Later that day Sierra and I hugged Demetri and Olivia goodbye.

"Don't go on any quests without us." Olivia said.

"Wouldn't dream of it." I said.

"I'm going to tell your father the whole story of our adventure, but I'll make sure he knows that I was the real hero." Demetri said, his head bandage was flopping on one side of his head as he walked away.

"I'm sure he'll believe you!"

I also hugged Maximus goodbye. "Make sure you keep Henrik out of trouble." I said.

"Thankfully that is not my job." Maximus said. "Oh, and I'm leaving you with a squad of my best soldiers to escort you back home—when you're ready. You'll have thirteen soldiers led by Captain Claudius. He is a man I would trust with my own life."

"I guess you'll be trusting him with mine for a couple of months."

When everyone was gone and Sierra and I were alone it finally hit me that we had come to the end of our quest.

"I'm a little sad it's over." I said.

"Septimus, this is just the beginning. The whole reason I traveled all that way to find you, and look what we accomplished! We actually succeeded in finding the sword and destroying the amulets before my parents launched an attack on the whole world." Sierra said. "And now you're here with me."

I nodded and smiled, but there was something troubling me. "What did your father mean when he said destroying the amulets would plunge the world into anarchy?" I asked.

"I don't know." Sierra said, and she gently brushed my face with the back of her hand. "I think my father would have said anything to stop us from destroying the amulets."

I pulled a large fragment of one of the amulets out of my pocket and inspected it. I had sent the rest of the fragments to Aracnash, but thought it wouldn't hurt to keep one as a souvenir. After all, it was my magic sword that had destroyed them, and I was the only one who could have wielded it.

Still, something was bothering me. Yesterday the amulets had exploded before my eyes, and now their evil power was broken. Yet I wondered, could this be what was preventing the end of the world?

Acknowledgements

This novel probably would never have happened if my older siblings, Danielle and Jakob, hadn't inspired me with their own creative writing and world-building. A huge thanks to my cousin, Lauren Larsen, who did the incredible cover art! Also thanks to my editors: my dad and my sister, Danielle Larsen, who has two published works of her own (artwork also by Lauren)! Thanks also to my mom who read it through one last time to help me find errors.

I owe thanks to all of my friends and family who encouraged me to see this through to the finish instead of being my usual lazy self! I would also like to thank my cats for their neurotic support (and an occasional typo when they walked across my keyboard).

Joseph, my brother: Tag, you're it! Go write a novel, and be quick about it. Pip pip cheerio, I say!

Made in the USA
Columbia, SC
27 November 2023

27216266R00083